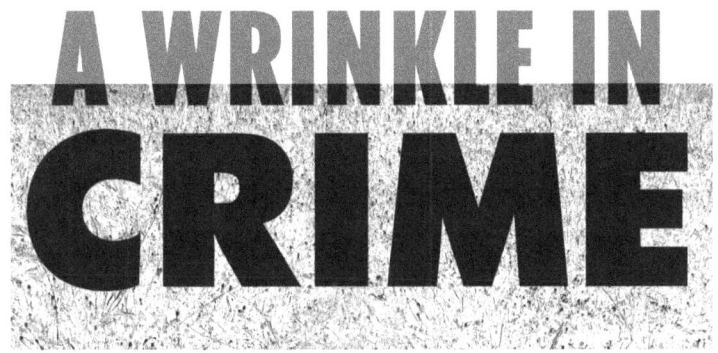

10 Stories of Foul Play, Murder & Revenge

I0553403

JOEL ARNOLD

Studio City Media Endeavors
Minneapolis, Minnesota 55378
www.studiocity.me
952.233.8088

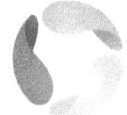

STUDIO CITY
media endeavors

This book is also available for eReaders.

For Judy & Mary; sisters-in-crime
and in-laws extraordinaire

Table of Contents

The Opportunity

Dale adjusted his glasses as Linda tried a different radio station. "It's all country music out here," she said. "All about having a beer with Jesus and exes living Texas. Yee-uck!"

"Why not pop in a CD?" Dale suggested.

"Tshh," Linda said—her usual off-putting response. As in—*Like I asked for your input.* Tshh.

"Well, turn it off, then," Dale said.

He concentrated on the road, or at least what he saw of it. At least it was a four-lane divided highway. That helped a little bit. Although the posted speed limit was sixty-five mph, he'd be damned if he took it over fifty. Not in these conditions. It was a white-out. Blizzard. You name it. The snow didn't so much fall as dance spastic dervishes in front of the windshield. If it were to simply fall, that would be one thing. But it blew up, down, sideways, and in circles. Disorienting. Hypnotic. It was hard to focus through the whipping sheets of snow. Dale kept finding himself staring at the big, thick flakes, following their patterns of lunacy as they danced across the windshield.

"Can't you step on it a bit?" Linda asked.

"Do you want to drive in this crap?" Dale replied.

"Do you *want* me to drive?"

"Ha," Dale said. "No."

"This has been the longest ride of my life," Linda said.

"I bet it's a lot longer for all those cars we've seen in the ditch."

"One car," Linda said. "One car in the ditch."

"Three," Dale countered. "Just because you didn't see them doesn't mean they weren't there." He sighed. "Why don't you just put the seat back and close your eyes. Try to sleep."

"I would if I could find some decent music."

Dale put a little more pressure on the gas in the hopes of appeasing her. They'd just dropped their youngest off at the university after a two-week long winter break. In good weather, the drive was two hours, mostly past farmland and forest, but tonight they'd already driven over two hours and they were barely halfway home.

"That's more like it grandpa," Linda said, closing her eyes.

Ah yes, *grandpa*. Whenever he drove, she always called him grandpa or gramps or even granny. But *he* never got speeding tickets. *He* never caused their insurance rates to increase.

The taillights of a van materialized a short distance ahead through the wicked swirl of snow. It was creeping along much slower than he was, and he knew if he didn't pass it, Linda wouldn't let up until he did. He tightened his grip on the wheel, signaled, and eased out into the left lane. The wheels skidded a bit, but held their ground. Dale focused ahead and finally passed the van in what seemed like an eternity or two. Only then, after putting the van some distance behind them, did he let out his breath and loosen his grip. But only slightly.

Alison was the younger of their two kids, and this was her first year away from home. She seemed to have adjusted to campus life quite well, the calls home growing less frequent as that first semester wore on. It was good to have her and David home for the holidays—David an accountant in Las Vegas, of all places—and now it was just the two of them again. A couple of empty nesters.

But...

A couple of empty nesters on the verge of—dare he say it? Think it? *Divorce*. Not so hard to contemplate when he said it out loud to himself a few times in front of the bathroom mirror. *Linda—I want a divorce*. He didn't look forward to what would come after uttering—no, *saying with conviction*—those words. But this week...Or next week, for sure. At the very latest, before spring break rolled around.

The kids would understand; he hoped so, at least. Surely they had felt the tension these last half-dozen or so years. The mostly silent, but occasionally loud, nasty tension. He knew there was more to life, and frankly, he sensed that Linda felt it, too. And so...

And so...

They weren't getting any younger. And they certainly weren't getting any happier.

Dale squinted through the mad reflection of snow in the headlights. There was a glow up ahead. It grew larger, and finally Dale made out the shape of a snow plow moving slowly in the left lane, its many bright lights caught in the bubble of snow that danced around it. Its plow created a massive wall of snow that it pushed off to the left, into the wide median, but in this weather, with the wind blowing so hard, the wall of snow wasn't neatly corralled. Gouts of it flew in every direction, and the plows lights and Dale's headlights turned the spinning snow on both sides of the plow into opaque white sheets.

Dale slowed and eased in behind the powerful vehicle, keeping a good distance behind its wake. Thirty miles and hour. Dale adjusted his glasses. Well, looks like this drive just got a bit longer, he thought. To get around the plow meant that he'd have to pass it on the left and hope the plow didn't decide to change lanes at that moment, since surely the driver wouldn't be able to see Dale's sedan sneaking past him. It also meant he'd have to drive through the blinding wall of snow and ice the plow kicked up, taking a leap of faith that he'd come through the other side free and clear. Driving through that wall of icy debris the plow and wind churned into the sky was literally driving blind; if a deer happened to be on the road, or God forbid, a stuck vehicle, then that would put a quick stop to *this* little jaunt home.

He glanced over at Linda, expecting—no, hoping—that she was already asleep. Instead, her head was turned toward him, eyes on his eyes, and that little smirk on her lips as if to say, *You don't have the guts.* She said nothing—not with words, anyway—and merely faced forward once again and closed her eyes, while that smirk, that stupid *you don't have the guts, gramma* smirk remained.

He tightened his grip on the steering wheel. Took a deep breath. Focused. He was already in the right lane, so now he just had to go for it—you don't have the guts—just go for it, step on the gas, put the pedal to the medal for a few brief moments, and take that leap of faith. Break on through to the other side, as the Doors used to sing, and then she couldn't call him gramps or gramma. At least not *this* night.

He forced his foot down on the gas. Drove into that blinding, furious wall of whiteness.

When Dale came to, he had no idea how much time had passed. He only knew it was still dark out, and that he was upside down, and something dug painfully into his chest and gut. The seat belt. Of course. He realized his glasses were no longer on his face, and that the car's interior was almost pitch black, and what little he could make out was blurry. A cold stream of air caressed his face. Something in the car had broken. He knew that the windows had been rolled up tight, the heater on, and now somehow the cold air was entering the car stinging his cheeks and making a moaning clarinet-like sound.

What *time* is it? It seemed like something important to know. But there was no glow from the digital clock readout, no lights on in the car whatsoever. The engine must've died. What the hell?

Then he remembered his daughter. Oh god, was she... no, they dropped her off at college, and then there was the highway and the snow and then...

The plow.

And—

"Linda! Oh, God, Linda!" he gasped. He turned his head slowly to his right. It hurt to do so, but he didn't think anything was actually broken up there. He saw her silhouette. She was also strapped in and upside down, gravity tugging at her long hair.

Dale cleared his throat. His tongue found a hole where his front teeth had been. "Linda?"

She didn't answer.

"Linda!"

He sensed movement. A groan. "Yes," she groaned. "What...what happened?"

Dale spat a small glob of blood from his mouth. "I don't know, exactly. We were passing a plow, and..."

"Jesus," Linda said.

"Cell phone?"

Linda didn't answer right away, but he heard her moving. Searching? "Ow. Geez, I hurt," she said.

"Your smart phone—can you reach it?"

"I don't know. I—ow. It hurts to move. What about your phone?"

"It's—I think it's in my pocket, but I can't quite—if I could get this seat belt unbuckled, then maybe..."

He found the buckle's release button and pressed it. The thing was stuck. But wait. There. He felt the shape of his smart phone in his jean's front pocket. It would take some work, but maybe...

He couldn't get his fingers inside his pocket, but if he

pressed on the edge of the phone through the denim, perhaps he could coax it out that way just enough so that he could grab it. He felt the bottom edge of the phone through the outside fabric of his jeans and pressed at it, trying to force it to slide out.

There. It gave slightly. But...but...

"Linda? How are you doing?" he asked.

She didn't answer.

"Linda?"

Another moan. "I think I'm hurt pretty bad," she said.

"Are you—is anything broken? Are you bleeding?"

"I don't know. It's kinda hard to breathe."

Dale suddenly wondered if he was okay. He hurt, especially where the seatbelt pressed into him. But he didn't think anything was broken. What about internal damage? Can that be felt, he wondered. His nose dripped. He touched the tip of his tongue to the moisture. Blood. A nosebleed. Well, that wouldn't kill him. It would stop on its own, wouldn't it? The space where his front teeth had been didn't seem to bleed any longer.

He tried untucking his shirt to use it to press against his nose, but the damn buckle held it tightly in place. He tried lifting his left arm up to his face so that he could press that against his nose, but limb seemed to be asleep. He tried flexing his fingers.

There. The feeling of pins and needles as blood flowed back into his hand was painful.

How bad is Linda, though?

He heard her breathing. Labored breathing. He turned

to look at her again. His eyes were adjusting to the darkness, but without his glasses, she was still blurry. And her hair covered most of her face.

"The plow," he said. "The driver must've seen us go off the road. I'm sure he called someone."

Linda didn't answer.

He envied her in that at least she had kept her winter coat on. He couldn't stand keeping his own on while driving, especially with the hot air blowing. His coat was in the back somewhere, his gloves in the pockets of the coat, his knit winter cap (that Alison had made him as a sophomore in high school) was stuffed in one of the sleeves.

"Linda?" he said.

"Stop," Linda said.

"What?"

"Stop asking me if I'm okay. It hurts to talk."

"Okay."

He could slide the phone out if he really tried, but…

There was this nagging thought. At first he tried resisting it, but he let the thought out a little at a time, let it surface in his brain bit by bit just to see how it felt. Like when he first started thinking of the D-word.

And the way it felt scared him. Because the thought felt sort of—

Sort of *good*.

He could slide the phone out if he really tried, but he said, "I can't get my phone out. It's really stuck."

Linda groaned.

"I'm trying, but it's so damn tight in there."

How bad was Linda, really? Did she need to get to the hospital right away? Was this a life or death situation?

That nagging thought…bit by bit…

It was so damn cold. His breath came out in gray wisps.

If she needed a doctor, how soon did she need one? *Really* need one?

And here, that nagging though that felt a little too good…

Could he wait her out?

It would sort of make things easier in the long run, wouldn't it? He knew that if he asked her for a divorce at some point, she would not just go gently into that good night, as the poet once said. No, it would be bitter. Costly. But this way…

There's the insurance money. And the kids, they'd be sad, sure—devastated, even. But at least they're grown up, now, and at least *this* way, he wouldn't be the asshole. Well, not in their eyes, or the eyes of the public. Because all anyone would know was that it was an accident. And it was an accident. It wasn't murder, really, if he just outlasted her, was it? At least not in the eyes of the cops.

Especially if his hand…

He took a deep breath, raised his right hand and punched at the windshield as hard as he could. He felt something break. Not the windshield—his fingers. And the pain, of God, it hurt. He didn't know how many he'd broken, but ow, ow, ow, God, it had to be enough, didn't it?

"Jesus, what did you do?" Linda asked.

Dale tried keeping the pain at bay. He felt fresh blood

drip from his nose, he felt lightheaded, and the pain in his hand blossomed into something he'd never quite felt before. Oh, God that fuckin' *hurt!*

"I—I couldn't feel my hand," he lied through gritted teeth. "I was trying to get some feeling back into it. I didn't think I hit the window so hard."

An opportunity; that's what it was. How many times had Linda accused him of squandering perfectly good opportunities?

Well, not this time, Linda. Not this time.

The feeling in his left arm slowly, painfully came back. He flexed his left hand. Damn, it was cold in here.

"How are you doing?" he asked again.

She didn't answer. How long did he need to wait? Just 'til morning? 'Til daylight revealed their overturned car? Would that be enough time?

He shivered. Tried to say, "I love you," but couldn't summon the courage for such a simple, yet blatant lie. Not now.

It wasn't murder, was it? Outlasting her wasn't really murder.

Was it?

Otherwise growing old and outlasting the spouse you no longer loved through natural causes would be murder. A much slower, more devastating murder. A double homicide.

Dawn started to creep into the sky. It infused the fallen snow with a calm glow. The wind had died, the snow stopped falling. Everything was so still.

Linda looked over at Dale. It was finally light enough to

see him, to really see him. Frost had formed over his face and slid across his dead, staring eyes.

Linda sighed. She finally—easily—switched on the smart phone she'd been holding all night, keeping it warm. The signal was strong.

She dialed 9-1-1.

Opportunities like this didn't come around every day, and this one had been a doozy.

"Hello," Linda said, making her voice sound a bit worse than it really was. "We've been in an accident."

Taking Care of Katrina

This is the only communication you'll receive. If you ever ask me about it, I'll deny everything.

To think he'd almost pawned his Blackberry an hour before receiving the email.

My grandmother doesn't seem to want to expire. She's not long for this world, but why should I wait? Get the picture?

It was a proposal. A set of instructions. Sent from a co-opted account with no contact info at all. But he knew right away whom it was from.

Johnny Billings. Not only heir to his grandmother's millions, but also Bruce Gavin's number one drug buddy.

So this is what I want you to do.

The instructions were simple, and simple was a good thing.

Meet her at the drop-off point. Tell her you're filling in for Gerry. She'll arrive on a Metro Mobility bus.

The drop-off point was where all the busses dropped off their passengers for the fair.

She'll be in an electric scooter with an Elvis bumper sticker across the back.

Elvis?

Bruce Gavin scanned the seniors getting off the bus.

She'll be wearing a pink windbreaker and pink cap with Elvis bedazzled across the bill.

Bruce wondered how many pilgrimages she'd made to Graceland. What was it about Elvis and old people?

Well, better Elvis than Barry Manilow.

She's old. She's going to die soon, anyway. You'd be doing her a favor. And you could use the twenty k, right?

Johnny had been right about that. Twenty grand would get his head above water. Now he'd have some feed money to win his whole body out of water. Never mind that the casino was where he'd gotten in trouble in the first place.

Twenty grand. He could pay off his dealer. Pay off a few other small debts.

But could he go through with it? He'd never killed anyone before, never even considered it.

But twenty thousand dollars?

The risk was minimal, the instructions simple.

There. She was the last one off.

The driver lowered her in her electric scooter to the pavement. Bruce stepped up to her and took a deep breath before introducing himself. Luckily, they'd never met.

"Mrs. Billings?" he asked.

He'd tried his best to blend in. Khaki shorts, an orange and brown striped bowling shirt, a pair of new bright white athletic shoes. And for just the right touch, a pair of white sweat socks that rode up his calves and ended just below the knees.

"Yes? And who might you be?"

"I'm Bruce. Gerry's replacement. He's home sick, I'm afraid."

The old woman scowled at him. "Gerry's a girl."

"What did I say?"

"*He.* You said *'He's* home sick.'"

Bruce shrugged. "*She's* home sick." He grinned. Thought best to make light of his error. "I'm getting old."

"Don't patronize me." Katrina Billings sighed. "Gerry loves the fair. I hope it's nothing serious?"

"No," Bruce said. "Nothing serious."

Although maybe it had been something serious. The email had promised Gerry would be taken care of, and that could've meant anything.

There was part of the email, however, that bothered him.

Let her enjoy her last day on earth. Take her where she wants to go. Let her eat whatever she wants to eat. Let her live it up. Who knows, maybe she'll keel over by the time the day's through without you having to do a thing.

Why wait? Why not just get it done and over with?

But it would be easier to blend into the crowd after dark, easier to walk away from an old woman slumped over in her scooter.

Elvis fan or not.

He looked down at the old frail woman in her electric scooter with her pink windbreaker in this eighty-degree heat. Hard to believe she was worth millions.

"So where to?" Bruce asked. He'd never been to the fair.

"I always start off with the animals," Katrina said. "I love the smell of hay in the morning."

"Smells like victory?" Bruce joked, referring to his favorite movie. When she didn't respond, he said, "Okay, which way?"

"Who doesn't know where the barns are? Perhaps you should've picked up a map."

"Or you could just tell me."

Katrina tilted her head to look him in the eye. She studied him for a moment. Then she shook her head. "Take a left."

Johnny Billings was a spoiled little shit. Bruce knew that. But he also knew that it was good to have a rich friend. Especially a rich friend who'd would soon get a hell of a lot richer. They'd known each other since high school. A private school. Johnny got in due to his money and family name, Bruce because he was smart. He'd done well in school, at least until his senior year when he discovered the wonders of a few select drugs. There'd been pot, a little meth, and a lot of coke. He loved coke, and Johnny always seemed to have some. After high school, Johnny began to turn to the harder stuff. Started snorting heroin. Even got into a little fentanyl, which was some dangerous shit. Bruce steered clear of that. Stuck with good ol' coke.

Bruce figured that Johnny liked him because, A—he put up with Johnny's bullshit—the lies, the bragging. And, B— because Bruce was built like a brick shithouse. His hulking presence caused people to think twice about trying anything stupid.

Bruce followed Katrina through the barns. She seemed particularly enamored with the poultry barn. Bruce had never seen so many damn chickens in his life. And then there were the sheep. And the cows. And the pigs. Katrina insisted on seeing them all. She talked to them. Cooed at them, told them how pretty or handsome they looked. Tell them she'd take them home if she could, and let them live out the rest of their lives in peace.

What B.S. Johnny had told him stories of how ruthless Grandma Billings could be. How she kept threatening to cut him out of his rightful inheritance if he didn't shape up.

Well, there were worse things Bruce could be doing. Following an old lady through rows and rows of livestock might not have been his idea of a good time, but at least there'd be a payoff when it was all said and done.

Bruce and Johnny hadn't been in contact for months, and Bruce had heard a rumor that there'd been some intervention orchestrated by the very woman he was now escorting between rows of rabbits. The same woman who was now telling a pair of rabbits how wonderfully fluffy their little fuzzy-wuzzy tails were.

Last he'd heard, Johnny was in rehab drying out.

Last he'd heard, that is, until he received the email.

They maneuvered to the horse barn. Everything going fine until Bruce stepped in a big pile of horse crap hidden beneath a mixture of sawdust and woodchips. It curled up around both sides of one of his brand new shoes.

He cursed under his breath and tried to shake the offending material off.

"Is there a problem?" Katrina asked.

Bruce nodded at his shoe. "I stepped in a problem."

Katrina glared at him. "I have been unable to walk for quite some time, now. I'd say you're rather lucky that you still have the privilege of stepping in anything at all."

Ouch. Score one for Granny Billings, Bruce thought, sighing.

Bathroom break. Finally. He rolled her to the entry of the women's bathroom, unsure of what he was supposed to do. "You, ah, need any—"

"I can make it." Katrina drove herself through the bathroom door.

Bruce entered the men's room and locked himself in one of the dark green stalls, the paint etched with crude drawings and epithets. He pulled a small vial out of his pocket and poured a tiny amount of white powder onto his finger. He snorted it into his right nostril, leaned back and closed his eyes, letting the brief rush hit him. God, he'd needed that. For a while, he thought he'd never get the chance. Perhaps now he could make it through the rest of the day without losing his mind.

He checked his watch. 12:21. He wiped the sweat off his forehead and tried to remember the rest of the email.

Go to the ring toss. There will be a package waiting for you. It will say FOR LEROY on it. Inside will be half of your reward. You'll receive the rest after the funeral. There will also be a little something to sprinkle on Grandmother's mini-donuts. Save it for after dark.

"How about going to the midway," Bruce suggested.

Katrina clapped her hands together. "For once, we're on the same wavelength."

"Great. Which way?"

"You're certainly a bright one, aren't you?"

He followed her terse directions and soon they were there. "Smell that?" Katrina asked, breathing deeply.

Bruce breathed in and shrugged. Fact was his nasal passages had seen better days.

"That's the smell I love. That's the smell of youth and innocence. That's the smell of the fair."

"Yeah?"

"Hot grease, cotton candy, cigarette smoke, diesel fuel––a combination like no other place on earth. If that smell could be bottled, I'd take a lifetime supply."

Wouldn't need much, Bruce thought. Now to find the ring toss.

They were surrounded by games of chance, thrill rides, and food stands. So many people. So many vibrant colors. *So many young women in shorts and bikini tops,* Bruce thought. As he followed her whirring scooter, the Elvis bumper sticker sparkled in the hot sun. Carnies on either side vied for their attention.

"How 'bout winning something for granny," a young man called out to them. "Come on, she deserves a prize."

"The carnies here have gotten so neat and tidy," Katrina said. "It wasn't that long ago when there wasn't a mouthful of teeth to go around the bunch. Now they're all clean-cut youth with their nice red shirts. I can't decide whether to buy a pronto pup, or let them do my taxes."

The carnie persisted. "C'mon, man, play a couple rounds for gramma."

Katrina called to the man—a boy, really—"I can win my own prizes, thank you."

"All right!" said the carnie. "A feisty one. C'mon, then. Take a few shots."

She aimed her wheelchair toward the young man's booth, the Temptress Toss.

"Mrs. Billings," Bruce said. "You don't really want to play that, do you? I mean—it's a rip-off."

Katrina's scooter stopped abruptly and she slowly turned her head. "A rip-off is spending one of my last times at the fair with a stranger who knows nothing about me." She faced the Temptress Toss again. The young man watched them, silent now, his mouth agape. Katrina's scooter inched forward. "This is *my* day," she said. "Don't ever tell me what I can or cannot do."

"Okay," Bruce said. "Sorry."

He waited, his hulking form behind her as she threw a set of balls at a pyramid of red, white and blue blocks. She missed and handed over tickets for another round. Then a third round. The carnie looked at Bruce and shrugged. Bruce wanted another snort of coke. Or at least a cigarette. Hell, what he really wanted was for Katrina Billings to knock over the damn blocks so they could get on with it and find the damn ring toss game.

Katrina dug through her purse. Her shoulders slumped. "I used up the last of my tickets. We can move on now." She pulled out a twenty-dollar bill and handed it to Bruce. "Get us another set and let's find something else to blow them on."

Finally, finally, the ring-toss.

"This looks fun," Bruce said. "Why not try your luck here?"

Katrina studied him a moment. "If you insist." She traded tickets for a bucket of plastic rings. While she tossed the rings at the tightly bunched glass bottles, Bruce nodded to one of the carnies. A guy with close-cropped bright red hair walked up to him.

"You got a package for Leroy?"

The carny's face lit up. "I was wondering what that was all about. Hold on a sec." He walked to the other side of the booth, reached under a ledge, and pulled out a stuffed animal—a cute brown wolf. A piece of blue painter's tape stretched across its back, and in black marker was written 'Save for Leroy'. He handed it to Bruce.

"That's it?" Bruce asked.

"As long as you're Leroy."

Bruce clutched the stuffed wolf and stepped back over to Katrina, who continued to toss red plastic rings at glass bottles.

"Getting any?" Bruce asked.

"I'm not through, yet," Katrina said. She tossed another ring. It bounced off a bottle, flipped into the air and landed around a bottle's neck. She perked up. "What do you know?"

* * *

In the restroom again. In the dark, claustrophobic stall. Bruce stared at the stuffed wolf. As he examined it, he took another snort of coke. A wolf. A stuffed wolf. He turned it over in his hands. Shook it. Sniffed it. There was something off in the stitching around its neck.

He tore the head off and poked his fingers through the neck and into the stuffing. There. He felt something. A big wad of something. He pulled it out. His heart raced at the sight of it. Hundred dollar bills in two tight rolls. A fresh wave of euphoria ran through him. He counted the rolls out. Fifty bills in each. Ten K. Half the money.

So this was it. This was real. He hadn't been completely sure until then. The possibility that the whole thing was some big joke had nagged at the corner of his mind this whole time, but now...

Now...

The email had promised the other half after the funeral.

He could walk away now. Ten thousand dollars was a nice chunk of change. Just walk away, no blood on his hands and be done with it.

He sat there, sweating. Looking at the money. In the middle of each roll was a small packet of white powder. On each packet was a laser printed label. One said "For Katrina" while the other said "For you—but not until it's over." Bruce laughed. *Like anyone would know.* But he still had enough of his own to get him through the rest of the afternoon and into the evening, so if Johnny wanted him to wait, he'd wait. He held the packet marked 'For Katrina' up to the fluorescent light that reached over the stall. He opened it carefully, wondering what exactly it was. It was a finely ground white powder. He sniffed at it. No odor to speak of, at least none he could detect. He wondered if it was a crushed percopop, some major shit he'd only tried once—something Johnny was quite fond of, however. He held the other packet up to the light and smiled. Johnny knew what he liked. Had to be coke.

You can do this, he assured himself. His heart fluttered. His breathing grew rapid. *You can do it.*

Besides, he couldn't run away. Not yet. He needed the other half of the money. He could do this. He had to. He hadn't been sure before, not really sure, but now, with half the cash in hand (never mind the fresh snort of coke working through him) he could do it. Easy. Easy. Then go. Take a vacation. Go to the Bahamas or Mexico or, hell, go to Vegas.

He closed his eyes, took some deep breaths, forced himself to calm down. He stood in the cramped stall. Shoved the bills deep into the front pocket of his shorts and dropped the rendered wolf behind the commode. He flushed for good measure.

"Are you all right?" Katrina asked when he emerged.

"Sure. Why?"

"For a moment, I didn't think you'd make it." She leaned forward in her scooter and held out a tissue. "You've got a little powdered sugar under your nose."

He took the tissue and quickly wiped his upper lip.

He followed the slow moving scooter down Judson Avenue and up Underwood Street, where Katrina stopped in front of Ye Olde Mill. "This is older than I am," she said.

"What is it?"

"It's a tunnel of love."

He watched her looking at it, staring longingly at the sign, at the paddle wheel that churned eternally through the strange chemical blue water. "You want to ride it?"

She shook her head. "I'm much too old."

"C'mon," Bruce said. "It'll be fun. I'll help you."

He watched her fight back the urge to say no, the urge to tell him she didn't need any help, the urge to tell him she could do any damn thing she wanted all by herself, thank you very much. But instead, she looked up at him, her eyes moist, and nodded. When their turn came, he lifted her from the scooter and set her in the back of one of the boats.

She was lighter than he expected. He squeezed in next to her.

The boat wound its way through a maze of impenetrable water, and soon entered a tunnel where the light disappeared. Bruce strained to see, but the darkness was complete. He couldn't even see Katrina next to him, although he felt her slight frame pressed against his.

"Sure is dark," he said. "I've never been in such a dark place."

After a moment, Katrina whispered, "I have."

Bruce almost asked her what she meant, but the boat gently turned and dim light surrounded them. He glanced at Katrina, who clutched her small purse and stared straight ahead. When daylight flooded the small boat, the ride was over. Bruce quietly lifted Katrina from the boat and gently set her back in her scooter.

* * *

They crossed Underwood to the Agricultural Building. They moved through the bright building slowly, and Bruce watched Katrina admiring the produce, the bars and cookies, the jars of honey butter and honey jam, red, white and blue ribbons displayed alongside them.

"Did you ever enter something in the fair?" Katrina asked softly.

"No," Bruce said. "Can't say that I have."

"Never created something you were so proud of that you wanted the world to see it?"

Had he? Had he ever created something he was proud of? Maybe when he was a kid and he'd been into models; World War II fighter planes—the Curtiss Helldiver, P-47 Thunderbolt and Supermarine Spitfire. He remembered the smell of the airplane glue, the sticky feel of it on his fingers as he fit the tiny pieces together. And there was the model paint, dipping his brush in the small glass bottles and carefully spreading the colors across the plastic, giving the pieces life. His hands had been so steady back then. Now, not so much.

Yes, he *had* created something he'd been proud of, but that had been so long ago. And then he and his friend Charlie Cameron had shoved firecrackers into the cockpits and blew them all to shit in his backyard.

"Not for a long time," he said.

Katrina shifted in her chair, craned her neck to look at him. He felt her eyes on him, and he returned her gaze with half a smile before looking away. She said, "I won half a dozen blue ribbons before I got married. This was at the Olmsted County Fair, mind you. Not the big time, like here."

* * *

"Yeah?"

"Twice for cookies—molasses crinkles. Three times for jam—apple rhubarb in consecutive years—and I would've had a fourth win if Betsy McCollum wouldn't have gotten a hair up her rear. And once for apple pie. But," she waved a finger at Bruce, "what I'm most proud of creating are my children. Both of them are dead now, one in an auto accident, the other lost to cancer. But Stanley, the one taken by cancer, had a son. Johnny. So in a way I created him, too. He's got some of my genes, at least. If only he'd stay on the straight and narrow." Her voice trailed off, but Bruce felt her eyes on his, even after he had to look away, after he couldn't stand those eyes of hers burning a hole through him.

Finally, dusk came.

It was time.

He followed her through slow moving barricades of people, the throngs parting like taffy before her scooter. There. Mini-donuts. As she stopped to admire a group of children making spin-art, he purchased a baker's dozen. He stood next to a garbage barrel, pulled the packet marked 'For Katrina' out of his pocket and sprinkled it onto the donuts. He closed up the bag and shook it, spreading the powder through the bag, coating the fresh, hot donuts.

They passed a band shell, and Bruce chuckled as he realized the polka band there was playing a surreal version of a Nirvana song.

"What's over there?" he asked, pointing toward a cadre of truck trailers.

"Let's take a look, if we must."

He handed her the bag of mini-donuts.

She took them. Looked up at him. A smile crept over her features. "Why thank you," she said.

As he led her between the trailers, he noticed with relief that there was hardly anyone back there, and the large trailers blocked the direct glare of the streetlights.

Katrina pulled a sugary donut from the bag and placed it in her mouth. She chewed slowly. She blinked.

Bruce stood over her, watching. He realized he was barely breathing. Jesus, what was he doing? How had it come to this? He had the urge to knock the bag away, to shout at her to spit out her mouthful of poison.

But the money. The money.

What had he become? What had led him here?

He pulled the other packet from his pocket. If he had to watch her die, make sure she was dead, at least he could make himself feel a little better. He dipped his pinky in the packet, lifted out some of the white powder, and snorted it up his nose.

He watched Katrina reach in the bag, pull out another donut, pop it in her mouth and chew.

She said something so quietly, that he wasn't sure if he heard her. "Sorry?" he said.

"I said they named a hurricane after me." She looked up at him, chewing. "Mr. Gavin."

Now he was confused. How did she know his last name was Gavin? When did he let that slip?

She tossed another mini-donut in her mouth and

chewed, a twinkle in her eyes. She seemed to waver. Bruce rubbed his nose. Everything seemed to waver. It grew hard to breathe, and his heart tried to beat its way out of his chest.

Katrina stopped chewing for a moment. "You don't look so well," she said.

Bruce tried to talk, but his tongue felt as if it had grown a thick rind of bark.

Katrina leaned forward in her chair. "I know my grandson is anxious for his inheritance," she said. "But he knows full well he gets nothing until he's thirty. Even if I die right here, right now, Mr. Gavin. *Thirty.* That's six years from now. I don't expect to live that long, so why would he want to risk killing me?"

Bruce blinked. There was two of her now. No, four. The sweat that poured from his face felt like tiny army of insects crawling down his skin.

"*He* knows that. And I know that," Katrina said, her voice a low warble. "I just want him sober by then. And with friends like you, how can he ever hope to clean himself up?"

Bruce couldn't get air into his throat. Something dripped from his nose. Blood?

"Mr. Gavin. I'm old. But I know how to use a computer. I know how to send an email. 'B Gavin twenty-five at b-l-g dot com. Sound familiar?"

She popped another mini-donut in her mouth. "Mmmm," she said. "Thanks for the powdered sugar. It adds a nice extra bit of sweetness."

* * *

She rode her electric scooter slowly down the midway once more, admiring the lights, the sounds, the smells. She breathed in deeply, closed her eyes and held it all inside as long as she could. It brought her back to her childhood when things were simple and the burdens of the world were still so far away.

She rode through the exit and spotted her limo. She slid off the scooter and stood—she'd borrowed it from her friend, Joyce—and stretched. It felt good to be on her feet again.

"Have a nice time, Mrs. B?" Gerry asked, opening the door for her.

Katrina Billings sighed. "I've had better days."

Gerry frowned. "I wish you wouldn't have gone alone."

Katrina smiled. "I can handle it."

"I know that."

"How about you and I come back here tomorrow?"

"I'd love that, Mrs. B."

"I would, too, Gerry. I would, too."

Hole in the Fence

"What have you gotten into, now?" I knelt down next to my dachshund, Hilde, steadying her upper torso with one hand while trying to get hold of whatever it was that was sticking out of her mouth with the other. A few desiccated black feathers. I pried her jaw open and pulled out the remains of a dead crow. I grimaced as I realized it was not a fresh kill—it must've been rotting for a while before my only companion for the last four months had found it.

I scolded her. "Dead birds don't make good chew toys." Her furiously wagging tail disagreed.

A few months ago, after getting her from the animal shelter, I would have worried about her getting sick, but this was the third dead creature she'd brought home in the last month—ever since the thaw. The first had been a frog, then a week later a tiny black vole. She didn't have much interest in eating them, just carrying them around for a while until I caught her and pried the poor dead things out from her jaws. And so far, at least, she'd been just fine.

"Hilde!"

She was loose again. I'd let her out in the backyard—the *fenced-in* backyard—but there she was, running around happy as a clam in the street out front. It was my own fault that she wasn't very well trained. I admit to spoiling her with table scraps and her own spot on the bed next to me. But she understood the pain I was going through, the loneliness.

Okay, I guess that's a lie if you get right down to it; there was no way she could know why I was lonely any more than I could understand why she liked to carry old dead things in her mouth. But I believe deep down that she—like all dogs—could sense the different moods of men and women.

It's no use calling after her. She'll let you get within a few feet and then take right off again, like it's a game to her. I worry about a car hitting her, or the Johnson's Rottweiler down the street deciding to use *her* as a chew toy. Hell, a large enough *bird* could carry her away.

"Hilde!"

She waited at the front door for me an hour later, filthy and reeking. I guess it was time to examine the fence. It was a wooden privacy fence that had come with the house when Linda and I moved here fifteen years earlier; big cedar planks stained ochre. Since Hilde was too small to jump the fence, there had to be a hole somewhere—perhaps a board missing or broken. But with the thaw, our backyard had turned to a mud pit, and I'd avoided the inevitable repairs.

I picked Hilde up and took her to the tub, rinsing off bits of dead leaves and dirt with the detachable showerhead. I shampooed away the awful odor that clung to her fur. "What have you been into?" I asked.

An awful thought crossed my mind, but I swallowed it deep. She was just a little dog after all.

I scooped her shivering body into a towel and rubbed her dry, ran my fingers gently over her sleek body, examining her from head to toe. She turned her head to lick my face, and I let her, but the smell of her breath nearly made me gag.

Just a little dog.

"Better brush your teeth tonight," I told her, looking for the small canine toothbrush the vet had given me.

I figured I'd best start chaining her up when I let her out back—at least until I could mend the fence. But that night she woke me out of a deep sleep with a volley of sharp yips. I'd been dreaming about Linda again, about that night she'd left me for good, and it was hard to let that go. I stumbled to the back door in my boxers and t-shirt and let Hilde out without thinking much about it. I waited for her. And waited. And then I remembered about that damn hole in the fence. "Hilde!"

Hell…

I dropped onto the couch, my eyes drifting shut, until I heard scratching at the back door. I stood, yawned, probably scratched some part of myself, and let her in.

Filthy again and she stank to high heaven. "What's that you got in your mouth this time?" I asked.

I knelt down groggily and pried her jaw open as her thin tail whipped back and forth.

A finger dropped to the hardwood floor. A blackened, rotting human finger, the flesh peeling from the bones.

I stared at it, trying to hold back the bile threatening to rise from the depths of my throat.

"Hilde," I whispered, absently petting her sleek fur. "What have you gotten into?"

I found a flashlight. Pulled on jeans, a flannel shirt, black jacket, workman boots and a black woolen cap. Grabbed a spade from the garage. I decided it was best if I left Hilde inside the house for this.

There's no real path through the woods behind our house, but Linda and I used to love traipsing back there when autumn had turned the maple and birch leaves into flaming yellows and reds. But it looked different at night, the trees skeletal in the early spring with their bare branches letting droplets of starlight bleed through. I stepped carefully, shining my flashlight here and there, trying to orient myself. I smelled the stagnant pond close by, ripe with the spring run-off, and I smelled something else, too.

Finally, I found it. Nearly tripped over it in fact, but stopped myself just in time. Linda's hand protruded grotesquely from the earth. The middle finger was, of course, missing.

I barely held back an anguished cry, but a small tear managed to escape, sliding warmly down my cheek and growing cold at the corner of my mouth as I jabbed the business end of the spade into the forest floor. I scooped up dead leaves, twigs and dirt, and piled them on top of her hand. I continued to scoop dirt over the shallow grave until it was no longer so shallow, and Linda, my wife who had "run off to Italy to be with another man" was once again secure beneath the weight of the fecund soil.

When I got back inside the house, Hilde greeted me, tail wagging furiously as she tried to lick the dirt from my hands. I knelt down and let her lick my face. "Hilde," I said, patting the top of her head. "I do believe it's about time we fixed that fence."

I guess the spring run-off had been worse than I figured.

Leave No Wake

I leaned against the gas pump stationed at the end of the dock and sipped from a lukewarm bottle of orange juice. Benny Helstrom's hail-pocked aluminum canoe pulled silently up. "How're they hitting today?" I asked, nodding at the half-dozen turtles crawling over each other on the floor of his canoe.

He tossed a loop of rope around one of the pilings and shook his head. "Sons of bitches are scarce as shit today, Mr. Varney. Scarce as shit."

I realized long ago that there was nothing stopping the vulgarities that tumbled from the eleven-year-old's mouth, so I'd long since given up. His mother worked two jobs, and his father had run out on them when he was only five. Besides, the kid was good at heart. If I've learned anything from my seventy-two years, it is the importance of keeping things in perspective.

"What'll it be this morning?" I asked.

"The usual." Benny held out two crisp dollar bills. The town of Nisswa paid him a buck per turtle for the weekly turtle races, and at the end of each race day, Benny gathered them up and released them back into the wild.

I waved the bills away. "Keep 'em." I walked over the aluminum dock planks and up cement steps sunk into a small rise of land. On top was Arrow Point Resort's lodge, a brown wooden building that served as shop, front desk, and owners' quarters, the owners being me and Noah Johnson. We had eight cabins for rent, plus space for some RVs and tents. Aside from the playground, shuffleboard, and a small beach with diving raft, we offered the most beautiful sunsets this side of the Mississippi.

The screen door slapped shut behind me, and I noticed that the cash register drawer stuck out like a squared-off tongue. "Noah!" I called to the back room. "Drawer's open. Again." I heard nothing in reply, but there looked to be no cash missing, the thin piles of bills arranged tidily in their appropriate slots.

Not only was Noah my business partner of thirty years, he was also selectively hard of hearing. He'd turned eighty the previous month, and if I recall correctly, he'd turned eighty the previous year, as well. For the most part, the older residents of Nisswa thought of us as a couple of old bachelors, but I think deep down they had us figured out, and that was fine with me.

Besides, we had the only boat-gas pump for miles around; boaters pulled up to the dock, filled their tanks, and then walked up to the shop to pay. More often than not, they bought a soda, beer, ice cream, maybe even night crawlers or a bucket of minnows. There's a whole mess of lakes up here, connected to each other by calm, quiet channels: Nisswa, Roy, Spider, Bass and Upper Gull Lakes, and of course, the enormous Gull Lake. We were on an isthmus dividing Bass from Upper Gull, and our dock jutted out into a section of narrows edged with water lilies. Boats passed slowly by whether or not they stopped for gas, heeding the *Leave No Wake* signs on either end of the channel.

I shut the cash drawer with a sigh, reached into the glass display case for a pack of bubble gum, and retrieved a cold Mountain Dew from the fridge. Back at the dock, I handed them to Benny and helped push his canoe off into the still, morning water.

"Thanks, Mr. Varney. I'm tired as shit today."

I nodded and waved as the foul-mouthed turtle boy disappeared amidst the water lilies and the glare of the rising sun. The smell of wet turtle lingered in my nostrils, so I inhaled deeply, filling my lungs with the scent of lake, pine and gasoline, bracing myself for the day.

The McMahon family from Duluth checked in just before noon, over two hours early.

"We don't have the beds made up, yet," Noah, fresh from a nap, informed Mr. McMahon, while his wife and two teenaged sons waited in the car.

McMahon grinned. "Don't bother. We bring our own linens."

Noah looked confused. "We do wash our sheets every day."

"It's my wife," McMahon said. "What can I do? She's

seen *Oprah* a few too many times—worried about germs."

"We only got good germs around here," Noah insisted.

"No offense. It's just the wife…"

My back was to Noah while I restocked the cigarettes, and I turned just in time to see Mrs. McMahon get out of the car carrying a bucketful of Pine-Sol, Lysol, Tilex—you name it. She set the bucket on the hood of the car and searched through it until she found a bottle of mosquito repellent, which she sprayed over her body.

McMahon noticed me looking, and shrugged. He arched his eyebrows as if to say, "Told you so."

A pair of fishermen checked in next, dressed in waders, camouflaged fishing vests and caps with slogans of beer companies stitched above the brims. Jim Blanchard and Chuck Regal. Jim was the smaller of the two, with huge, brown muttonchops peppered with stray crumbs.

"How's the fishing?" he asked.

Noah ran Blanchard's credit card through the machine. "The northerns are nibbling, the bass are biting, the perch are prodding, but the walleyes, by all accounts and estimations, are withholding."

I stepped up next to Noah, kicking him lightly behind the counter. "The fishing's fine," I reassured the two men. "The fishing's just fine."

Michael and Lynette Perry, twenty-something newlyweds, arrived next. The groom had called ahead and ordered champagne and a box of truffles from the Chocolate Ox to be waiting on their bed. The wedding occurred two days previous, and the glow on their faces and new gold rings had yet to wear off. The back window of their SUV still held traces of soaped letters.

"Sunset should be a nice one tonight," Noah said. "Should peak around eight-oh-seven."

The Perry's smiled indulgently at Noah and took their key.

Late afternoon, I shook out a small handful of pills from a plastic container divided into the days of the week and handed them to Noah. The container was supposed to help him remember to take his pills each day, but I'd become part of the dispensing equation years ago when it became apparent that Noah rarely remembered what day it was. He swallowed the pills two at a time, chasing them with swigs of iced tea. He cocked his head and nodded towards the door. "Someone's coming," he said.

The screen door opened and closed, and the scent of perfume, cigarettes and beer preceded the lone woman who entered.

Her name was Gina Veale, and we learned later that she came from one of the strip clubs out on Highway 10. But that afternoon, she hoisted a brown leather purse onto the counter and dug through it, pulling out a wad of crumpled tens and twenties. "I'd just like to stay a few nights."

Noah wrinkled his nose at the condition of the bills and carefully straightened them out, facing them the same way and placing them neatly into the register. I slid a registration card over the top of the counter, and after she filled it out, I handed her the key to cabin ten.

She tapped an unlit cigarette on the counter and looked out the screen door at the narrow one-way dirt road that led here.

"You all right?" I asked.

She looked at me for a moment. "I used to come up here when I was a little girl," she said. "Before my daddy died." She smiled, and it seemed like a hard won smile. "In fact, I remember you," she said.

I looked at her closely, trying to remember, trying to reconcile her face with any of the thousands of children who had stayed here over the years, but I couldn't place her. She had a narrow nose and dimpled chin, dishwater blonde hair and a yellow tank top that revealed the tattoo of a broken heart between her shoulder blades. On the small of her back was a series of Chinese characters.

Noah had a faded SEMPER FI on his left bicep, but his do-or-die days now consisted of tending the lodge and rocking on the porch, scanning the Nisswa Dispatch obits to reassure himself he was still alive.

"Sorry to hear about your father," I said. "Mine's gone, too."

Ms. Veale squinted at me, and I figured it had been a stupid thing to say since at my age, of course my father was gone. I coughed lightly into my fist. "I'm glad you decided to give us another try. If you need anything, let us know."

Aside from our renters, there was a slow but steady stream of customers needing gas for their thirsty boats. The fishermen, Regal and Blanchard, came in to buy a case of

Bud, and a short time later they left in a red pickup, probably to hit the bars in Brainerd or the casino in Hinckley. The McMahon teenagers bought ice cream sandwiches and Cokes and rented a paddleboat. Both were clean-cut and skinny, the older of the two sullen, the younger one wearing a perpetual smirk. The father had been in the shop earlier asking about local golf courses, and the mother—I figured she was holed up in their cabin cleaning, scouring and disinfecting the germ-infected rooms. I chuckled.

Noah spent most of the afternoon napping in the living room behind the shop. His relationship with his afternoon naps was much more torrid than anything he and I shared together. And when he wasn't napping, he often sat on his recliner listening to old vinyl records of Count Basie and Duke Ellington. They popped and hissed, but the sound was warm, like the saturated hues of an old Technicolor movie.

The way his mind had deteriorated in the last few years, I sometimes wondered how much time we had left together, how much quality time. But no matter what, I'd be there for him, like I knew he'd be there for me if things had been turned around.

I needed some fresh air.

I raked the small patch of beach and swept the docks, circling the property, picking up stray pieces of litter as I went. Some might call it puttering, but I'd never admit to it. I checked the fish-cleaning house, making sure the counters were spic and span, then checked the small hut where we kept our live minnows in a bath of running water.

Everything was good, including the weather, and I saw

Gina Veale sitting on a wicker chair on the redwood deck of her cabin, looking out across Bass Lake, a cigarette in one hand, a beer in the other. She looked hungry and lost and sad.

"Is there anything I can get you?" I offered, standing on the slope of shore next to the deck.

She slowly looked over at me and shook her head. "No," she said. "Thanks. Everything's just fine." Then she pointed to the lily pads that stretched out from the shore. "When I was here as a little girl, I caught a couple of turtles out there. I put them in my daddy's minnow bucket. Gave them names. Timmy and Tommy. Funny I remember that. Timmy and Tommy Turtle. But then I had to let them go before we left." She smiled thinly. "I cried," she said. "I really wanted to bring them home."

I nodded and smiled, not knowing what to say. But she waved a ring of smoke from her face and said, "Maybe they're still out there. Do you think so?" She took a sip of beer. "Timmy and Tommy."

She watched me expectantly, as if she really wanted me to remember her, and I tried, I really did, but how many kids had I seen here? How many little girls? And to transpose one of those small hopeful faces onto *this* adult? It just wasn't possible.

"You have a good night," I said, and walked quietly away so as to let her be with her memories.

The trouble started shortly before the sun readied itself to set on Upper Gull. A family of loons warbled close to shore, turtles poked their heads up between the water lilies, and bullfrogs started warming up for their nightly keening.

A black SUV set high over fat wheels slid to a stop on the gravel driveway in front of our shop, and a man in a tank top and Bermuda shorts got out, sunglasses hiding his eyes, short-cropped hair sticking up through a layer of sweat and gel. He stopped short of our door when he spotted Gina smoking outside her cabin. He turned toward her.

"Hey!" he called.

Gina tossed her cigarette when she saw him and turned toward her cabin's door, knocking over an empty beer can.

"Gina, wait, damn it!"

"Stay away from me," she said.

"Wait! Gina!"

"Fuck off." For some reason, she couldn't get her door open.

He jogged toward her. "What do you think you're doing? You think you can just run away? You didn't think I'd find out where you went?"

"Leave me alone." She got the door open and slid in, but when she tried to shut the cabin door, he wedged his foot against the jamb and reached inside, yanking her out by her upper arm.

I figured it was time to get involved. "Let go of her!" I shouted.

The man pulled her toward his truck and I stomped toward them, waving my hand in the air. "Stop that right now. What do you think you're doing?"

He ignored me as he opened the passenger door and

shoved Gina roughly inside. He slapped her across the face. I grabbed the back of his collar and yanked as hard as I could. "Leave her alone!"

The man spun, seeming to notice me for the first time. "Fuck off." He turned back to Gina. I grabbed his arm, and this time he shoved me hard. I fell flat on my rump. The air escaped me in a rush, and my chest tightened painfully. He slammed the passenger door shut and circled to the driver side while I sat in the dirt trying to catch my breath. It was when he got the door open and situated himself in the driver's seat that Noah fired a round of buckshot into the open car door.

"Let her go!" Noah demanded, shuffling purposefully toward the truck and leveling his old Winchester M12 at the man.

He raised his hands in the air. "You shot my car!"

Gina scrambled out of the truck and helped me gently to my feet. She called to Noah, "He took my purse."

The man called from inside the truck. "She works for me. It's my money. She stole it."

"Hand it over," Noah said, circling cautiously until he was only a couple feet away from the man.

"She's nothing but a titty dancer," the man said incredulously. He emptied the purse onto the passenger's seat and threw the empty purse out the window. "There. Take it."

"Give me my money!" Gina yelled. "It's all I have."

Noah said, "Hand it over or I'll shoot."

The man stared at Noah and the gun. He slowly reached down and turned the key in the ignition and gunned the engine, keeping his eyes on Noah the whole while. A smile played slowly across his lips. "You think I'm afraid of an old faggot?" He spit at Noah, hitting the end of the shotgun, and for a moment, I cringed as Noah's finger jiggled on the trigger. But in the end, there was no gunshot, and the man in the truck peeled away, spewing small stones and twigs and dirt behind him.

Noah lowered the shotgun and stared at the ground. Then he shuffled over to me. "You okay?" he asked.

My voice trembled. "I'm okay."

He looked up at Gina. "Sorry I didn't get your money back."

Gina wiped at her eyes and sniffed. "It's okay," she whispered.

"I'm going to go lay down for a while," Noah said. He walked slowly to the lodge. I followed him, feeling the eyes of our guests upon us. Once inside, I gently took the gun from him and helped him into bed. I locked the shotgun back in its cabinet and wandered out to the sunset bench.

The sunset bench was forty-feet long and sat halfway down the small slope of hill on the west side of our humble isthmus, positioned to catch the varying hues of salmon and nectarine and crimson that filled the sky and spread like spilled oil over Upper Gull each evening. I hadn't been out to see a sunset in a while, and now I needed to sit and let the rich colors fill and calm me.

Mr. McMahon sat on one end of the bench, his arms spread out on the backrest. His eyes shone. "By golly, that was some excitement. You get that kind of stuff up here a lot?"

I shook my head and chuckled. "Nope. Not much happens up here except maybe somebody has a bit too much to drink, or they play their music too loud, maybe shoot off fireworks in the middle of the night." Then I asked, "Are you enjoying your stay?"

He crossed his legs in front of him, bright white socks pulled up over his calves. "You've got a beautiful place here."

I nodded.

"You got any kids?" he asked.

I looked out at the distant trees, the sun melting into the branches. I gave a barely perceptible nod.

McMahon grinned.

"Your kids seem nice enough," I offered.

He shrugged. "Ah, heck, they're great. But sometimes a man needs to get away."

We sat in silence for a long while as the world quickly darkened, and before long, a gibbous moon floated in the sky. There was the sound of frogs and the gentle lapping of water against the shore. Muffled voices from the decks and porches of homes edging the lake carried through the air, and soon there was another sound that reached us.

The sound of crying. It came from down the shore, and slowly grew louder. Soon, a figure appeared, accompanying the sound. McMahon and I remained silent as Gina Veale neared, and we watched as she stopped to gaze out over the water. She reached into a pocket. There was the sound of a lighter being engaged, a small burst of flame, and soon the smell of cigarette smoke reached our nostrils. In her other hand, a beer can glistened with condensation. She wore shorts, her yellow tank top and flip-flops. She passed by, oblivious to our presence, and soon the darkness swallowed her.

McMahon broke our silence. "Poor girl," he said. "Poor girl."

That night I lay in bed next to Noah, my arm draped over his sleeping form. When I finally fell asleep, it was deep and hard and dreamless until the sound of an outboard motor pulled me back. I sat up and listened. The boat traveled fast through the narrows, and soon after it passed, waves slapped angrily against the pilings, and the moored boats knocked and thudded against the docks.

"Damn kids," I mumbled and fell back to sleep.

That morning, I noticed the lock on the pump hadn't been attached. Inside the shop, the gas meter was still on. A pending sale waited on the register. I quickly opened the cash drawer and checked the neat piles of money. It seemed to all be there. But in order to unlock the pump, a key was needed, and the key was below.

In all the commotion of the previous night, had I forgotten to lock up the pump? I tried mentally to go through the motions of the night before, but I'd locked up the pump so many nights for so many years, the same act over and over that it came back as one blurred act, and I could not distinguish last night from any other. *Getting as bad as Noah,* I thought.

The shop door opened. Regal and Blanchard, the two fishermen, walked in, dressed for a day of fishing. The sun was minutes away from bleeding over the horizon, and the sky was a hazy peach.

"Did you hear anything last night?" Blanchard asked.

"Like what?" I asked.

Regal elbowed his buddy. "Jim here is always hearing things."

"I heard a boat speed through the narrows in the middle of the night," I offered. "But other than that…"

Blanchard shrugged. "Thought I heard someone yelp. Like a short scream, kinda."

"Can't say I heard anything like that."

The fishermen paid for one of the fourteen-foot Lund boats, and I signed out number four, but I'd be damned if I could find the key. I crossed out the number on the rental agreement and wrote in a 'three'. At least *that* key was there. Wouldn't be the first time something around here hadn't been put back in its proper place.

I escorted the fishermen out to the boats, carrying a pair of life-vests for them while they carried the rest of their gear.

Not only was the key to boat number four missing, but the boat was gone as well.

"Noah! Damn it," I muttered.

I assured the fishermen that they needn't worry, and got them on their way. I stomped up to the shop. Noah stood at the register, yawning and scratching his chest. "Morning," he said.

I scowled at him. "Number four is gone."

"What d'ya mean?"

"I mean someone stole it."

"You sure?"

It wasn't the first time one of the boats was taken. They normally ended up along the shore, victim of a joyride. Sometimes the borrowers were even kind enough to sneak them back to the dock.

"I'll call the sheriff," I sighed. As I called, Noah stepped out of the shop, and came back in soon after.

"The girl's gone."

"What girl?"

"You know. The titty dancer."

"Her name's Gina," I scolded. "But what do you mean she's gone?"

"Her door was open a crack. I looked in and she's not there."

I called back the sheriff to tell him to forget about it; we'd figured out where the boat was. The dancer's car was still parked outside and her belongings were still here, so we figured she probably checked the boat out herself.

"She's just out for a ride," I told the sheriff, relieved. "She'll show up soon enough."

I stood on the shore staring out at the water lilies, the heads of turtles poking up now and then for a peak at the rising sun. Benny, the foul-mouthed turtle boy, paddled up to the dock thirty minutes later, the floor of his boat crawling with turtles.

"Sons of bitches are fidgety today," he said.

"That right? You want the usual?"

Benny carefully scanned the water's surface. "I'm needing

about a dozen more of these bastards before the races today. What the hell's wrong with them? Hey, can I get a Dew and a pack of gum?" he asked, holding up two ones but keeping his eyes on the lake. "Come on, you bastards," he whispered to the still water.

I pointed to the east side of the isthmus where the water lilies lay drenched with sun. "Seems to be a bunch of the bastards over there," I said.

I trudged back up to the shop and got his bubblegum and soda, and by the time I came back to the dock, Benny had maneuvered his canoe among the bright green lily pads, nudging them gently aside with his paddle. His method of turtle entrapment was simple, yet effective. Once he was near enough, he'd stealthily slip his paddle beneath an unsuspecting turtle and scoop the thing up and into his boat before it had time to figure out what had happened. But now he seemed to concentrate on something; a pair of turtle heads poking up next to his boat. They were still and he was still and I wondered what he was waiting for. All he had to do was scoop the things up, and he'd have two for the price of one.

Benny swallowed. He backed up quickly, the boat wobbling violently with the sudden movement. He stood, pointing at the turtle heads, and sat down hard when the boat threatened to tip.

I waved to him. "You all right? Benny?"

He grabbed his paddle and shoved it into the water, back-paddling with frantic strokes, trying to turn the canoe around. I looked closer at the turtles he'd left behind, realizing they hadn't moved this whole time. I squinted at them against the nectarine sun.

"Shit," Benny said. "Shit, shit, shit."

I barely heard him as it dawned on me that maybe they weren't the docile heads of turtles, after all. As a matter of fact, the more I stared at them, the more they looked like a pair of fingers reaching out above the water's placid surface.

"There's someone in there," Benny gasped. "Some lady. I saw her down there. Some lady."

I helped him out of his canoe, and he kneeled on the dock, staring out at the vegetation where the fingers poked out.

"Noah!" I hollered up to the shop. "Call the sheriff. Tell him to get down here as fast as he can."

It was Gina. A diver was called to retrieve her body from the lake and search along the rocky bottom and among the green stalks of lily for evidence. An anchor had been tied around her waist, but the water was only five feet deep where she'd been dropped, and her fingers were just long enough to protrude from the surface.

I talked to a deputy about the man from the strip club who'd come for his money, and who tried to take her with him. I was angry at not calling them earlier when the incident had happened. I gave a description of the man and of his truck, and Noah, amazingly, had remembered the license plate number (perhaps because it was **B88BS**). I also told them about the missing boat, and the boat I'd heard speeding through the narrows in the middle of the night. Was it our boat?

They questioned Mr. McMahon and the fishermen and the newlyweds, and they didn't have much else to add, other than the short, sharp scream Blanchard thought he'd heard. Mrs. Perry thought she might've heard a scream, too, or maybe it was a grunt, she wasn't really sure.

By the time they were done taking everyone's statements, the sheriff received a call on his radio that they'd apprehended the strip club owner. They found her money on him, and he was still dressed in the clothes he'd worn the previous night.

I tried to put it together. The strip club owner. He must've driven here in the middle of the night. Killed her. Put her in the boat and dumped her.

But he already had her money.

And why go through the trouble of hauling her to the other side of the isthmus to put her in a boat in order to take her back to the Bass Lake side, when that's where her cabin was? Wouldn't it have been easier to just carry her to that spot? Less risk of getting caught by someone out for a breath of fresh air?

But maybe she'd run from him, run to the Upper Gull side and that's where he killed her. So he put her in the boat, and…

But still, he had her money.

Maybe it was about more than money. Maybe he was a jilted lover, or…

But no, he said she worked for him. And he hadn't acted like a jilted lover, had he?

While I thought through all this, images kept running

through my head, images of all the young girls who had stayed here, all the girls I could remember, trying to conjure a face from the past and reconcile it with Gina Veale's world weary visage.

The next day, one of the residents on nearby Roy Lake called. Rosy Smith. She lived with her aging father in one of the many beautiful large homes that kept popping up all over these lakes. She said that one of our boats was moored on their dock. She said it had appeared the previous day, and she wondered when someone would come back for it, then noticed it had our name and phone number on it, so finally decided to call us. I drove down to their property with Noah, where we met the sheriff and one of his deputies.

Our Lund boat. The anchor was missing. No surprise there. But what *did* surprise me was the strong, familiar smell that wafted up from the boat's interior.

It wasn't until Noah and I drove back to the lodge that I placed the smell and realized what it meant.

Noah and I sat on the long wooden sunset bench facing Upper Gull and watched as the sun disappeared behind the trees, turning the sky a brilliant pink. I promised myself that I would do this more often, because this is what this bench was put here for, and I lived here, and why shouldn't I do this every evening? Besides, who knew how many more sunsets were left for me. Or for Noah. I let go of his hand when I heard footsteps clunk across the deck's wooden planks.

Mr. McMahon nodded at us, and sat down about five

feet from Noah. He squinted into the sunset and sighed. I watched him a moment, then asked, "Why did you folks decide to stay?"

"What do you mean? We registered for a week."

Soft, golden light dripped among the distant branches and spread like a slow fire across the water's surface. I kept my eyes on the lake. "Why did you do it?"

Noah slipped his hand back in mine and squeezed gently.

McMahon chuckled like I was some crazy old man. I looked at him. Stared at him. Stared until his smile faded. He said quietly, "You think I killed her?" He twisted the wedding ring on his finger.

Now Noah stared at him, too. "It doesn't really matter what we think," he said gently. "I'm sure they'll find plenty to make a case against you."

McMahon looked at us incredulously. His mouth opened and closed like a landed fish. "You don't—" he started. His head shook. "You don't know anything."

We watched him silently. Waiting.

He tugged one white sock up over his bare calf. Said quietly, "I tried to help her. That's all." He stood up slowly, brushing imaginary dirt from his shorts. He turned to look back at the cabins and sighed. Then he chuckled. "Why waste my breath on a couple old queens like you, anyway?"

Noah's voice shook. "Try us."

McMahon said, "I thought she could use some money."

I frowned. "So you gave it to her out of the kindness of your heart?"

Noah grunted next to me.

"Like I said, you two wouldn't understand." He sat back down on the edge of his seat and rocked back and forth, elbows on knees, hands cupped together. "Geez," he muttered. "Jesus." He blinked. The sun danced delicately on ripples of water stirred up by a cooling breeze. Finally he looked up at us. His voice caught in his throat. "My wife found us," he said, waving a hand at the Lunds pulled up on the shore. "We were in one of your boats. Mary's usually a heavy sleeper, but that night…" He shook his head. "She found us in the boat, and she just picked up the anchor and hit her over the head. It happened so fast."

His words sunk in, and my heart seemed like it had filled with a thick sap. Noah leaned back and turned his face up to the sky, his mouth hanging open, his tongue smoothing over his teeth.

"We had to get rid of her and the boat," McMahon said. "We took the boat out and tied the anchor to her. I didn't realize the water was so shallow. I tried to sink the damn boat, too, but do you know how hard that is? To sink a boat? We tried filling it with water, and I tried, but I just couldn't do it. So Mary decided we had to at least clean it, hopefully get rid of any evidence. So she went and got some Pine-Sol, and we scrubbed it out."

That's what I had smelled in the boat. The Pine-Sol.

"We each took a boat and followed each other, left one boat on someone's dock and sped back here with the other one." He looked at each of us in turn. "It was an accident. I was just trying to help her." He turned his palms up. "I just thought she could use the money."

"Where's your wife," I asked, realizing that I hadn't seen her or his kids all day.

"They went back home. She couldn't stand to look at me, and she took the kids back home and left me here without a damn car." He chuckled nervously. "So if either of you guys are heading to Duluth…."

Neither Noah nor I smiled.

"Look," McMahon said. "That man they arrested—that *thug*—he deserves to be in prison. Right? He should be there. Not me. Not Mary. Besides, that girl, Mary probably did her a favor. Look where she was headed. What kind of life was she going to lead?"

Noah and I slowly stood, our hands still together, and we walked past McMahon, heading up the small slope of hill to the lodge. We went inside, and I held onto the screen door to stop it from slamming, and then Noah held me, and my face was on his shoulder and I couldn't stop the tears; partly for the loss of Ms. Veale's life, but mostly because I had a sudden memory.

Gina Veale when she was seven.

I remembered.

I remembered.

Her standing on the shore while her mother and father waited, and she set down the turtles, one at a time, tears streaming down her soft cheeks as she waved goodbye to the slow, ambling creatures.

I remembered.

She looked up and saw me watching her, and she looked at me questioningly as if asking me to save them for her, to keep them safe, and I remembered.

I remembered smiling at her and winking, as if to say, *Of course I will.*

Was it only the first of so many lies and disappointments she'd have to endure?

And then she was gone and the memory was gone, and I could not stop the tears.

Finally, Noah pulled away from me. "I'll call the sheriff," he said. He reached out and gently rubbed the back of my neck. His forehead touched mine. "Let's get up early tomorrow," he said. "Let's watch the sunrise together."

I nodded. Yes, I silently agreed. We should watch the sunrise and the sunset as often as we could. Who knew how many we'd have left?

The Cheater
*a drabble**

She stood at the top of the steps, trembling, trying not to let the noise coming from the basement get to her. It was torture listening to a grown man scream—even if it was her husband. "That's what happens to cheaters," she whispered.

You don't cheat on your spouse.

Ever.

Another raw scream from below. She felt John's hot breath on her neck, and she turned into his arms.

"He won't last much longer," he said.

"I can't take it anymore."

John chuckled. "Consider it penance." He shut the door, muffling the horrid screams. "He never should've caught us."

* a drabble is a story that is exactly one-hundred words long, not including the title

Mercy

I live in a quiet neighborhood. Quiet unless you stand still for a moment and listen. There's the shrill of crickets and frogs by the pond out back. The raspy whistle of cars racing over highway 21. The leaves and branches of my sugar maple out front rustling in the wind. So many sounds, but there was once a time when those sounds all disappeared the moment I peaked out and saw Mr. Harvey Gale sitting there on his porch. Watching. Smoking a cigar. Drinking a glass of something or other. His eyes set on me like two hungry mosquitoes, searching for a spot to prick and have their fill of blood. Any sort of auditory stimuli disappeared, except for the creak of his damn rocker. That sound alone cut through the air, penetrated my skull and made me feel…unclean.

We live in a cul-de-sac. Our houses stare at each other across a wide street, the kind where in the winter, the plows pile the snow in the center, making a great white mound which would be the envy of any child—if there were any children living here. This particular cul-de-sac, whether by design or coincidence, has attracted only the retired or the childless.

I'm in the retired category. A widower. I have a daughter who lives in Seattle, and she has a daughter of her own. I follow her on Facebook, and I get the annual Birthday and Christmas cards, and I respond in kind. Wish I could say I miss her, and I'll probably be branded a terrible father for saying this, but she was a difficult kid, and her choice of husband…well, let's just say Birthdays and Christmases and Facebook give us our fill of each other.

I'd sometimes glimpse Mrs. Gale through a crack in their curtains, but to see her was a rare occurrence; an event to take note.

I'd see Mr. Gale all the time when he was home, puttering around his yard, pruning, weeding, cutting his grass with his riding lawn mower. Rocking on that chair of his.

But Mrs. Gale? It was as if she barely existed.

I avoided the man as much as I could, but our mailboxes clustered together at the corner of the cul-de-sac where it opens onto Clayton Avenue. It was inevitable that we'd fetch our mail at the same time. I used to say hello on those occasions to be neighborly, but after receiving only grunts in reply, as if my presence irritated him, I started saying hello just to annoy the mean old cuss.

One afternoon, however, when Mr. Gale was away fishing—I could tell because the old fishing boat he kept on a rickety trailer was gone from his driveway—I noticed that the Gales' mailbox was overstuffed, as if they hadn't retrieved it for quite some time. There's something about an untended mailbox that doesn't sit well with me, so I gathered it, took it over to their house, and rang the doorbell. After a bit, Mrs. Gale answered.

"Yes?"

I held her mail out. "Your mail," I said. "Not good to leave the box unattended. It's what the thieves and robbers of this world watch for."

"Do I know you?"

I was taken aback. Did she *know* me? "I'm your neighbor," I said. "Live right across the street over there." I pointed to my house and then offered my free hand. "Judd Malone," I said.

She nodded warily, and limply shook my hand.

"I didn't mean to cause you any alarm," I said.

She backed away, starting to shut the door.

"Your mail," I said, gripping the bundle. She hesitated a moment and finally took it.

"Mr. Gale out fishin'?" I asked.

She looked down at the doorjamb. "Please don't do that again."

"Excuse me?"

"You know what I mean," she said.

My smile faltered as she closed the door.

Despite her icy response, I noticed a couple of things. One was the shiner on her left eye. The makeup she wore was not quite enough to hide it. There was also the imprint of finger marks on her throat. She had her collar up, but it shifted when she moved, and the marks were clear as day. Deep red welts in the shape of big, bony fingers. It must've been terrifying; fingers around her throat cutting off the air. I wondered if she had thought she was going to die.

I had an older brother who used to wrestle me onto my back, hold me down, and press a pillow over my face. After a few moments as I struggled beneath him, he'd lift it off and yell, "Say it!"

I'd punch at him, scream, "Get off! Get off of me!"

But he was bigger. Stronger. He'd block my fists with the pillow, push it onto my face again, longer this time. "Say it!"

Panic. Always such panic. Black dots blossomed behind my eyes.

He'd lift the pillow.

"Mercy," I'd gasp, tears running. "Mercy!"

I don't know why he did it. A sense of power? Resentment of my being born, of taking away his status as only child? I never asked him, even after we'd grown and gone our separate ways. Funny thing is, we got along fine as adults. Only saw each other once or twice a year; Thanksgiving, sometimes Christmas at our folks' house while they were still alive.

My brother died ten years ago. Cancer. I went to his funeral, shed some tears. If I'm in the area, I'll stop at his gravestone and say a few words. Good words. We were both just kids back then. We both grew up.

But Mr. Gale…he was no kid.

He was a mean old bastard, through and through.

I had a dog, a mutt named Sweety Pie. She was a small thing, part Bichon, part poodle. I admit she was a bit of a yapper, barking at any old thing when I let her outside; dogs, cars, a slight breeze, dead worms.

Mr. Gale didn't like my dog. He called me more than once, telling me to shut her up. I apologized, of course. I shushed her, told her to be quiet, tried to distract her with a chew toy. But there wasn't much else to do to quell those tendencies.

One day the police paid a visit. Told me of complaints, neighbors calling in. The dog was too damn noisy. Made too much of a ruckus.

"There are other dogs in the neighborhood who are just as noisy," I told the officers. "Who was it?" I asked. "Who complained?"

They wouldn't tell me, of course.

"Harvey Gale?" I watched their faces closely.

The older one chuckled. "We can't tell you that."

But I saw it—a hint of recognition at the name, especially in the younger officer. It sure as hell was Harvey Gale.

"I'll try to keep her quiet," I said, knowing as well as they did that it was an empty promise. There was nothing to do about it, short of putting my dog down, and I wasn't about to do that. The thing was that however noisy Sweety Pie was, at least it was natural. The yelling, the screaming, the foul language I heard coming from the Gale house—that didn't seem quite so innocent—so natural. And it was always *his* voice raised. Always *his* voice unfurling a bolt of obscenities a mile long. Never *Mrs.* Gale's.

A week after the police stopped by, I received another call from Harvey Gale.

"You need to do something about that dog of yours."

I sighed. "It's a dog. A puppy. They bark."

"If you don't do something," Mr. Gale started.

"Then what?" I asked.

I heard him breathing. In and out. In and out. The rasping breath of a cruel old man.

He hung up.

I don't think it was the barking that really bothered Mr. Gale. I think it was an excuse. A reason to add a little more grumping and complaining to his miserable life. Or maybe he couldn't bear to see the affection, the love between Sweety Pie and me. Would he be happy if I kicked the dog? Beat it into submission? Would that sit right with his miasmic view of the world?

I found Sweety Pie in our back yard the next day. Dead. With no reason to be dead. I cried. Got down on my knees, picked her up, held her in my arms and cried. My tears soaked the fur on her neck and shoulders. I couldn't prove it—didn't have the resources—but I suspected poison. Why else would an otherwise healthy dog be yapping for joy one day and dead the next?

Had to be Harvey Gale. It only made sense.

Like I said, he was a mean old bastard.

Mr. Gale continued to rock away on his porch, smoke his cigar, drink his nights away. His rocking chair creaked its way into my bones like the onset of foul weather. His eyes twinkled with a pathetic victory.

But Mrs. Gale? Hardly a hint of her, except when their

car backed out of their garage, the mister behind the wheel, the missus in the passenger seat looking like the entire world was a rotten place to be.

So when I brought Mrs. Gale her mail that Saturday and saw the bruises, the marks left by strong, bony fingers on her neck, I knew I could no longer abide that meanness, that atrocity of a human being. I could no longer abide the ways of Mr. Harvey Gale.

I used a computer at the library in a nearby town to look up various sedatives. No use leaving a trail on my own computer—I watch those forensic shows. I know it doesn't matter how much you try to delete things off of your hard drive. They always find that kind of thing if they're looking.

So I used a sedative. Won't say what kind, because that's neither here nor there, but I filled a syringe and used *that* when I came calling. It worked like a charm.

I dragged the unconscious body to the car in their garage—the keys had been right there on their kitchen counter.

I wanted to hear him say it. I wanted to hear him say *mercy* after all he'd done; killing my dog, the abuse he'd inflicted upon Mrs. Gale.

I placed the unconscious body in the car, positioned it just so.

Mercy.

I wanted to hear him say it so badly.

I waited, staring at the body in the car.

I imagined him saying it, imagined his mouth forming

the sounds. *Mercy.*

I imagined his panic-filled eyes looking up at me, lips quivering over loosened dentures.

Mercy.

But my imagination had to do for now.

I started the engine. Shut the door. If there was an autopsy, they'd detect the sedatives, but that wasn't unusual for a suicide. I walked through the Gales' house and left out their back door.

A dog barked nearby. For a moment it sounded like Sweety Pie, but of course that wasn't so. I knew I had done the right thing.

That was over a month ago. I got a new dog from the local animal shelter. Another mutt, this one slightly larger than Sweety Pie; a mix of Welsh Corgi and I don't know what else. I haven't fallen in love with her as much as I had Sweety Pie, but we're still getting to know each other. The folks at the shelter told me she'd been abused by its previous owner. I'm slowly working my way into her trust.

She doesn't bark as much as Sweety Pie, but that doesn't matter to me. She can bark all she wants for all I care. Mr. Gale's not going to complain. He's not going to call me up at night telling me to quiet my damn dog. The cops won't come around to inform me of anonymous neighborhood complaints.

Mr. Gale ain't so mean anymore.

I know this because a week or so after the funeral, as I took my new dog out to do her business, I heard the creak of the rocking chair on his porch, heard it over the sounds of the crickets, the frogs, and the traffic on the nearby highway.

He was there on his porch smoking a cigar, drinking his glass of something or other.

When he saw me he raised his glass.

He knew who had killed his wife, but there was no way to prove it.

I could see it in his smile, see it in the way he nodded.

Mercy, that smile said. That nod.

Finally.

Mercy.

Blue-Eyed Mary

There's a group of sandstone caves in Rochester near the top of what is now a public park known as Quarry Hill. The caves were carved out in 1882 by inmates of the Second Minnesota Asylum for the Insane, led by a man named Thomas Coyne, who believed he was Jesus Christ. At one point, Coyne, a schizophrenic, carved the words to an old song on one of the cave walls, and although faded, they can still be made out to this day:

> *Come tell me blue-eyed stranger,*
> *say whither dost thou roam?*
>
> *O'er this wide world a ranger,*
> *has thou no friends or home?*
>
> *They called me blue-eyed Mary*
> *when friends and fortune smiled,*
>
> *But says blue-eyed Mary,*
> *now I am sorrow's child.*

Today, the cave entrances are blocked by iron, padlocked gates, but it wasn't long ago that they were open to anyone curious enough to enter. Teenagers hiked up to them after dark to get wasted, make out, or have a good scare. I know of at least two children conceived within those dark cave walls, but it wasn't until this year that I knew their names.

And I will confess right here and now to killing one of them.

Five months ago I balanced a tuna hot-dish in one hand and a bouquet of daisies in the other as I pressed the doorbell to my mother's house with my elbow. After a minute, I rang it again, the casserole dish hot on my palm. I'd only called fifteen minutes earlier from home, and knew she was expecting me. When she still didn't answer, I set the daisies down and tried the door. Unlocked. I entered, about to call out *Mom,* but saw her on the couch, crying. The only other time I'd seen her crying was when Dad died, and that had been over thirty years ago.

"What is it?" I asked.

There was the usual fragrance of orange and cloves; she still made the same pomanders that she did when I was a kid. I set the hot-dish on her dining room table, forgetting about the daisies outside the door. Something fluttered in my stomach. "What's wrong?" *Cancer? A brain tumor?*

She shook her head.

I leaned down and gave her a hug. "Come on. What is it?" I wiped at her tears with my knuckles.

She swallowed. "The news," she said, nodding at the

television. "There was a story…"

"About what?"

She picked up the remote and pressed the reverse button for the DVR. Images sped backward through a set of commercials and a portion of the evening news. "Here," she said. "This."

It was a story about the St. Paul Catholic Infants Home; an orphanage that also served as a home where young, unwed mothers went in secret to deliver their babies. It was known as Watermelon Hill by the local youth who thought the young women going in and out of the building looked like they carried watermelons under their dresses.

"I was one of those girls," Mom said. "My parents sent me there when I was seventeen. I was five months pregnant."

Although I'd grown up an only child, I knew I wasn't *that* particular watermelon. I asked stupidly, "Did Dad know?"

Mom shrugged. "I told him on our second date that I'd had a baby, but I didn't go into the details. He didn't seem to want them."

My father, Conrad Gordon, died of a self-inflicted gunshot in 1980. I was barely eight years old. He checked into a motel room with only a gun wrapped in a towel stuffed in a briefcase. A maid found his body. At the time, I was told it was a heart attack; I wasn't told it was suicide until I was sixteen. Mom showed me the gun, a Ruger Security-Six. I remember touching it, but I never asked why she'd kept it.

"What happened to the baby?" I asked.

Mom shook her head, fresh tears brimming. "They swaddled her up and let me hold her for a few moments before making me give her back. They told me it was for the best." Mom tried valiantly to smile through her tears. "She had such beautiful blue eyes. I'd carried her all those months, and that was all I got."

"I can't imagine how hard that must've been."

"It was the hardest thing in my life."

"Whatever happened to her?"

Mom shrugged. "I don't know. Adopted, probably. That's what happened to those children." She looked at me and patted my hand. "But then I had you. You are the joy of my life, and that what's important."

We sat down to the tuna hotdish. There were so many questions to ask. So many that I ended up not asking any at all. Not until later.

This morning, a high school senior found the body. He lived near Quarry Hill, and on early Saturday mornings he'd bring his alto sax to the edge of the old, abandoned quarry below the caves and play jazz. He told the news reporter that he liked the acoustics of the place, the way the notes echoed off the limestone walls. He liked to watch the sun rise over the hill, and told the reporter that he didn't notice anything wrong until the sun crested the hill. Then he saw something in the old blasting shack on the quarry floor. He went down to check it out and found a body slumped down in the shack, a leather jacket covering the head and shoulders.

I don't know how early the kid arrived at the quarry, but he probably didn't miss me by much.

* * *

It was impossible to stop thinking about what my mom went through as a teenager and how she'd kept it a secret for so many years. But most of all, I couldn't stop thinking that I had a sibling out there. Was she still alive? Did she know she was adopted? Would I meet her someday?

Not long after learning of my new sibling, I stopped by Mom's for a visit, armed with a bottle of her favorite white wine. I wanted information.

I pulled the cork and poured her a glass. She always kept a six-pack of beer for me in the fridge, so I grabbed a can and sat next to her on the couch.

"I don't really know how to ask this, but I can't help but wonder if that half-sister of mine is out there somewhere," I said.

Mom tensed as she sipped her wine. I guzzled half my beer and plunged head. "I want to find her."

She shook her head. "That's not a question."

I took a deep breath before finally asking, "May I have your permission to find her?"

It was Mom's turn to sigh. She rubbed her temples and closed her eyes. She took a long sip of wine, finishing off her glass. As I poured her another, she said, "She was my blue-eyed Mary long before I gave birth to her. That's what I'd call her when I talked to her in the womb."

"You knew she was a girl *before* she was born?"

She looked up at me, her eyes bright and wet. "I can't tell you how I knew, but I knew. I could picture her. And when I finally saw those blue eyes, I knew I was right. We had this special connection. Even after they took her away, even after it felt like a part of me died, I still *felt* her."

"But you never found out what happened to her? Where she went? If she's even still alive?"

She patted my forearm. "Before you were born, I still felt that connection. I felt I knew what she looked like, what she was doing, what her voice sounded like, what her moods were. Of course, when you came along, you took my full attention, but I still...*felt* her. My blue-eyed Mary. And yes, I feel that she's alive somewhere."

My spirits rose. "Let's find her," I said. "The both of us."

She shook her head. "I don't think I want her to know me."

"Why?"

"What if she had a bad life? It would be my fault, wouldn't it?"

"You were seventeen," I said. "A kid. Nobody's going to pass judgment on you *now.*" I thought for a moment. "How old would she be?"

She didn't even need to think about it. "Forty-six."

"What if I can find her?"

"It was a closed adoption, Michael. They don't just give that information out to anyone."

"Can I at least try?"

Mom looked at me, her eyes warm and sympathetic. "I just don't know if it's a good idea." She managed a smile and shrugged. "But I won't tell you no."

I wrote a letter to the Catholic Charities in St. Paul requesting information. I also sent a letter to be placed in the adoptee's file; a way to let the adoptee know that the birth mother was open for contact. Of course, I wrote it all in my mother's name, Donna Gordon, and put her return address on it so that any information would go right to her.

So when Mom called me a month ago and said, "I got something in the mail," I knew what she was talking about.

"I'll be right over."

Mom still lives in the same house I grew up in. Not much has changed, save for the framed photographs in the hallway where you can watch me grow up. Even then, the newest picture is from my college graduation over fifteen years ago. Once, before she retired from Mayo, I took the day off from work and spent it painting her living room. I thought the white walls could use an update, so I laid down a base coat first thing in the morning and spent the rest of the day adding a darker coat of taupe, daubing it with a rag to give it a faux-leather look. Tedious work, but I managed to finish just before she got home.

When she came through the door and saw me splotched with paint, she gasped and raised her hand to her mouth. It was like she'd just seen someone get hit by a bus.

"Surprise!" I said.

When I came for dinner two weeks later, the walls were back to white. She made no mention of it as she poked holes in an orange and filled them with cloves.

You think I would've learned.

But that day the letter arrived...

"I'm afraid to open it," she said.

I turned the envelope over in my hands. "We can't not open it." It was addressed by hand, the return address had the surname *Billings* with a Milwaukee address. I slid my finger under the envelope's flap, and paused slightly before pulling out the sheet of paper, waiting for Mom to object.

She sighed and shrugged. "Well?"

I unfolded the sheet of paper and read the handwritten letter. It was short and sweet.

Dear Donna,

Thanks for expressing interest in contacting me. I've been hoping for a long time that I might hear from you.

It went on for a bit longer, but...

"There must be some mistake."

Mom looked up. "What do you mean?"

This time I read the letter out loud to her, and when I got to the end, I read, *"Sincerely, Kent Michael Billings."*

Mom looked up. "What?"

"Kent Michael Billings," I said. "I'm guessing that's not a girl." Then I asked, "You *did* see her, didn't you? You're sure you had a *girl?*"

Mom reached for the letter and took it from my hand. Then she did something I was not expecting. She tore the letter into pieces. "I didn't have to see her. I knew. I always knew. It was a girl. And oh, such blue eyes. I wish you would've seen them, Michael."

So. Mom never *really* knew, did she?

Sometimes when you build up something so much in your mind…I realized that it had to be hard for her to accept that she'd had a son, not a daughter, but she'd come around eventually. And more important to me, I *had a brother out there!* And he lived in Milwaukee! An easy day's drive.

Growing up, I'd always wished for a brother, and even now, at thirty-eight years old, the idea of finding a long-lost brother was so…*exciting.*

Mom would come around.

I talked to him on the phone three weeks ago. He was just as excited as I was to find out he had a brother. He said he'd felt as if something like this might happen someday. And to think, his middle name was my first name!

Kent was twice divorced. No kids. Yes, he'd always known he was adopted. No, his parents never kept it a secret from him. More importantly, his parents were always good to him. Unfortunately, they were hit and killed by a drunk driver while he was attending his junior year at college.

The last thing I'll tell you about our conversation is that deep, deep down, he always felt he had a brother somewhere. We talked for over an hour, but here's the thing; I want to keep the rest of our conversation private. Because it's all I really have left of this newfound brother of mine.

The only other time I heard Kent's voice was when he checked into the hotel on the outskirts of Rochester on Thursday night and called to say he'd made it in safely. He was nervous, but looking forward to finally meeting me and his birth mother in person on Friday night.

* * *

Last night it was all over the news. The unidentified body found in Quarry Hill Park by the high school senior. All they knew was that it was a male in his 40s or 50s. He had no identification on him. The police asked for any information that might help identify the victim.

What they didn't say on the news that night was that the gunshot wound that killed him had obliterated his face so that their sketch artist couldn't even do a rendering of the man.

I turned off Mom's television and turned to face her. Tears flowed freely from my eyes. I put my arms around her. Squeezed her so tight.

"Michael? Honey? What is it? What's wrong?"

Two weeks ago I tried to convince her to just meet with him. He was so eager to meet *her*.

"I really don't want to talk about it," she said.

"But Mom—he doesn't blame you. He's had a good life, and if anything, he'd thankful that you gave him to such wonderful parents."

"I didn't give him to anybody. The nuns took my baby. *They* gave my baby away."

"You know what I mean," I said, exasperated.

She whirled around and stuck her finger in my face. "Listen to me," she said through gritted teeth. "I was raped in those caves."

I felt like I'd been slapped.

She stepped back, exhaling, and brushed away some imaginary lint from my shoulder. She lowered her voice. "I'm only going to tell you this once."

She told me how the boy she was dating al those years ago, Hank Beaumont, was tired of only getting to second base, and one night he took her up to the caves in Quarry Hill. Donna laid a blanket down on the dirt floor and Hank turned off his flashlight. They made out, their hands all over each other, but when Hank begged her to go further, Donna refused.

"Please?" he begged. "Just this once?"

Donna said no, but Hank Beaumont didn't take no for an answer that night in the caves of Quarry Hill. He pinned her down with the weight of his body.

"Afterward, he found his flashlight and turned it on, setting it on the ground so that it pointed at the ceiling. He got dressed quickly and told me to hurry up. I was hurt. Bleeding. I couldn't stop crying. I begged him to go and leave me alone. I couldn't look at him. I got dressed facing the cave wall and that's when I noticed the words carved there. A poem. I ran my fingers over them and read them in the dim light.

> *Come tell me blue-eyed stranger,*
> *say whither dost thou roam?*
>
> *O'er this wide world a ranger,*
> *has thou no friends or home?*
>
> *They called me blue-eyed Mary*
> *when friends and fortune smiled,*
>
> *But says blue-eyed Mary,*
> *now I am sorrow's child.*

"It was signed 'Coyne the Prophet.' At that moment, I thought he was talking directly at me, as if I was Blue-Eyed Mary. But I realized later that it wasn't me. It was the baby that started forming inside me that night."

Sometime early Saturday morning, a few hours before dawn, I drove up to the Quarry Hill picnic shelter with my lights off, following the glow of the half moon. The shelter was surrounded by trees, and there was no one else there. I parked as close to the trail that led to the caves as possible.

My half-brother was heavy. I dragged him a bit at a time, resting often. The sound of his shoes sliding on the dry autumn leaves on the wide trail seemed unbelievably loud; I felt like the whole city could hear us.

I intended to place him in the cave, under the verse chiseled into the wall by Thomas Coyne. *Coyne the Prophet.* But as I neared the cave's entrance, I discovered that it was closed, a locked iron gate placed across its mouth.

I was exhausted. I looked out over the quarry spread below me, the half-moon painting the limestone a dull gray. It would have to do. I steeled myself, whispered to his lifeless body, "I'm sorry, brother," and began to drag him once again.

But I'm getting ahead of myself.

Friday night I sat at a table in a restaurant in downtown Rochester. Kent Michael Billings was supposed to meet Mom at her home and have some time to get to know each other. Then they were to meet me here at seven. I checked my watch. It was now just past eight.

I called Mom's house, but got her voice mail. I ordered another beer and nursed it for another hour. Still no Mom. No Kent, no long-lost brother. I paid the bill and left. Maybe, I thought, they were so caught up in each other's stories that they'd forgotten the time.

Or maybe something was wrong.

I tried calling one more time, but to no avail. I drove to her house.

When I rang the doorbell my mother opened the door.

"Where's Kent?" I asked.

I smelled oranges and cloves.

Mom shook her head. "Who?"

"What do you mean, *who?* Where's Kent?"

"I'm here by myself," Mom said. "I was hoping you'd stop by."

I stared at her a moment before pushing myself past her into the house. "Did he call?"

"Nobody called," Mom said.

"He didn't call? Did you try the hotel?"

"What are you talking about?"

I grabbed my mother's shoulders. "Come on—don't do this to me. *Kent,*" I said. "Where is *Kent?* Your son?"

Mom reached up and brushed a strand of hair from my forehead. "You've always been my one and only son, and always will be. You know that."

There was blood on my mother's fingers. "What is going on? What happened to your fingers?"

She held up her hands and examined them. "I guess I got carried away with my pomanders. Those cloves can be sharp little buggers."

I walked past her into the kitchen. Where were these pomanders, these oranges and cloves that I smelled so acutely?

And just where the hell was my brother?

"Kent," I said again to my mother as I walked past her. "Let's stay on subject. Kent. The son you had forty-six years ago. The brother I invited here to meet us. Come *on,* Mom. This isn't funny."

I stood at the top of the basement steps. The oranges and cloves smell seemed to come from down there, but there was another scent that I couldn't quite place. It was like a piece of burnt toast, or…I couldn't place it. I hurried down the steps.

Dozens of oranges were set on the basement shelves, each orange studded with cloves.

Then I noticed my father's Ruger lying on the dark, shag carpet. That's what I had smelled—the discharge of a gun.

I faced the back of my dad's old easy chair six feet away from me. I noticed a hand on the armrest.

Oh, God. No.

I took three quick steps toward the chair and braced myself before looking down. It was Kent. Most of his face was gone, but I knew it was him—my long lost brother.

I felt someone behind me.

"A stranger," Mom said. "He knocked on the door, and I answered and he walked right in. I had Conrad's gun. I'd been looking at it earlier. I don't know why, but I had it with me. He tried to talk to me, tell me things. Things I didn't want to hear."

"Mom."

"He kept talking."

"*Mom,*" I repeated.

"He's a *stranger.* He's not my blue-eyed Mary. He's a *stranger,* don't you see?"

"Oh, God, Mom."

I barely caught her as she collapsed in my arms, sobbing. I held her.

"Okay," I said, patting her back. "We'll figure this out. We'll take care of it."

"*You're* my son," she cried. "You're my only son."

"Okay, okay," I soothed. When she felt steady enough, I eased her down onto a wooden chair. I picked the Ruger carefully up off the floor, emptied out the bullets and put them in my pocket. Then I found a bottle of white wine. "You go upstairs," I said, handing it to her. "Pour yourself a glass. I'll take care of…" I couldn't finish the sentence.

My brother.

I began to clean up, trying to think of the best way to deal with the situation. Maybe not the best way, but the only way that I thought possible.

Saturday, sometime before dawn as I dragged my brother down the path into the quarry, I realized that my mother had built up her first child in her mind so much, her blue-eyed Mary; she knew her, created her out of pain, regret, guilt, sorrow…necessity. She had tried to create something that might turn that night in the caves and all those days at Watermelon Hill into something…good.

I told you that I murdered one of two children conceived

in the caves of Quarry Hill.

I murdered her, murdered my mother's blue-eyed Mary. I murdered her by finding my mother's real child. Her other boy. Kent Michael Billings. The man I now dragged in starts and stops down to the old quarry floor. He deserved better than this. I know that. But I didn't know what else to do.

I placed Kent in the old blasting shack, a small closet-sized building of crumbling limestone. At least, I thought, it would protect him from the elements. I placed his leather jacket over his head. It seemed like the decent thing to do.

I thought about a lot of things that night, things about my father's death, suspicions that I'll never share with anybody.

I did my best to cover my tracks, but I'm sure I missed something. Seems like you can't even blink without some forensic lab finding out about it. But that's okay. If they connect the murder to us, I'll confess to this one, too. I'll confess that it was me and me alone who shot Kent Michael Billings. It's what an only son does for his mother.

Occupied

With each stride, Brenda Chapman's running shoes hit the dirt trail with a muffled, yet satisfying, smack. It was a hot, humid day at Cone Hill Park and Campground. Sweat blossomed across the front and back of Brenda's gray tank top. Her purple headband was soaked through. She dug in, straining, as the trail rose sharply. When she got to the top of the hill, she slowed to catch her breath, walking in a circle, checking her pulse. She glanced at her watch. So far, she'd made good time, and now it was downhill for a bit—at least until it was time to turn around and jog back the way she'd come.

She liked this trail. Not far from home, never crowded, and she was out in nature, damn it! No cars honking as they passed, no same-old, same-old of the suburbs in which she lived. There were some small drive-up campsites spread throughout the park, but they were rarely in use. And today—she couldn't imagine camping in this kind of heat. But jogging; that was another story.

She stretched, propelling her arms in circles, rolling her

head on her neck. No view up here to speak of, since the hill was covered in thick, leafy trees. But she liked the trees, and here their branches reached over the narrow trail, turning the sunlight into an overhead mosaic.

A thick layer of old, fallen leaves created a soft, earthy mattress just off the trail, and for a moment, Brenda imagined lying down on them. Just lay there and stare at the branches. But no, she thought. I'm a warrior princess! I'm goddamn Xena!

Besides, she had a wedding dress to fit into. Time to get a move-on!

She took a deep breath, checked her posture, and continued her jog down the trail. Her wedding was in a month and she'd already trimmed off the fifteen pounds she'd wanted to, so now it was all about keeping them off and working on her tone and stamina. Besides, jogging in these rolling hills was a great way to relieve stress. Gee-suz there was a lot of stuff to get ready for a wedding!

A forest-green fiberglass outhouse at the bottom of the hill marked her halfway point. *The Biffy Palace.* It stood on a circular gravel surface about twenty feet in diameter. A service road continued on its way behind the outhouse to the highway beyond.

Brenda usually just circled it, pretending to use its gravitational pull to fling her back the way she'd come. She'd seen that in a movie once, only it had been a spaceship flung around the sun, not a jogger flung around a pre-fab outhouse.

But this time she actually had to use it. She wasn't a big fan of small, confined spaces, but when you had to go, you had to go. As she neared, she noticed the small indicator just below the door handle was red. *Occupied.* That was a first. She considered just going off trail a few feet to pee *au natural,* but she figured with her luck, that would be about the time a troop of Boy Scouts came hiking along. She jogged in place, waiting.

When the door finally opened, a startled female looked out at her.

Brenda smiled, wiping sweat from her cheeks with the back of her wrist. "Hello," she said.

The other woman smiled back. "You scared me." She wore a thin pink dress and sandals. Long red hair spilled over her shoulders.

"Sorry," Brenda said.

"It's okay." The woman's face was beaded in sweat. She stepped out and stood in front of the outhouse.

Brenda wondered why she didn't step aside. She nodded at the outhouse door. "I need to—"

The redhead quickly moved aside. "Oh, geez, of course."

Brenda jogged inside and shut the door. Latched it shut. *Occupied.*

The sun shone through the fiberglass in a toxic-green glow. The venting slots near the low ceiling did nothing to relieve the stifling heat. The air was deathly still. Three distinct scents vied for the number one spot in Brenda's nostrils; the smell of human waste, of course, and trying to cover that was a pungent chemical odor—a strong disinfectant of some sort. It made Brenda's eyes threaten to water. And to top it all off was the cloying scent of vanilla—as if a hundred automobile air fresheners had been tossed inside this tiny fiberglass hut.

Aside from the competing odors, it was just plain hot in there.

An oven. Brenda pulled off a long length of toilet paper, wadded it up and mopped the sweat off her face and neck. She quickly peed, pulled up her shorts, squirted some hand sanitizer in her hands and pushed the door open.

Still sweltering outside, but at least the air was fresh and moving. However hot it was outside, the inside of *ye olde* Biffy Palace felt exponentially hotter.

She took a deep breath, bracing herself for the return half of her jog. The redhead she'd encountered earlier was nowhere in sight, and Brenda wondered if she was braving one of the park's shaded campsites.

She started back up the hill, looking forward to a nice long shower when she got home. *Looking forward to settling into Mark's arms in their queen-sized bed.*

Usually, Mark jogged with her, but today he'd said, "Not today. I love ya babe, but it's just too damn hot out there." Now, as she jogged her way back up the hill, she saw his point.

A sharp whistle startled her. A man shouted, "Hey! Hey you!"

She looked for the source of the noise and spotted him just off the trail about twenty feet ahead. She slowed. Stopped. Jogged in place.

"Yes?"

"I need your help." He wore jeans, a t-shirt, a baseball cap pulled low over a pair of sunglasses and close-cropped hair.

"With what?"

"It's my wife. Something's wrong."

Brenda grew wary. Something didn't feel right. "Where is she?"

"Just over here."

"I've got a phone in my car," Brenda said, keeping her distance. "I'll call for help."

"I already did that. They're on their way. But please—until they get here, I really need some help."

Damn it, if the guy really needed help, she'd hate herself for ignoring him. But still…something about him…

He was tall and lanky with ropey muscles. He wore a leather belt with a large knife sheathed on the side. A small strap of worn leather to keep the knife secure was unsnapped.

Was that it?

Trust your senses, Brenda told herself. This did not feel right.

She was about to apologize again, offer more help in finding more assistance, but as she opened her mouth, he leapt at her, pulling the large serrated knife from the sheath.

Shit!

She spun around and sprinted down the hill. She heard the man's footsteps behind her, heard him shout, "C'mere, bitch!"

Jogging down a hill was one thing, but sprinting in a near-blind panic was something else.

This isn't happening. This isn't happening, she told herself, her heart racing. Then—*Watch your footing.*

The man stumbled behind her; she heard him grunt, "Shit!"

She glanced over her shoulder. Had he fallen on his knife?

No such luck. He sprang up.

Don't look back again. You can outrun this guy.

But as she neared the bottom of the hill, neared the gravel surrounding the Biffy Palace, she realized he was fast. Very fast. She heard his breath come out in controlled grunts. He sounded much too close.

Her foot hit the gravel and slid out from under her. It wasn't much—she didn't fall—but a sharp pain shot up her calf. Damn it!

Should she try to outrun the son of a bitch? What if he caught up to her? What if he threw the knife and it caught her between the shoulder blades? The Biffy Palace loomed in front of her, looking like an oasis in a desert of gravel.

She jumped inside, slammed the door shut and slid the latch in place.

Occupied.

Just in time. He pounded on the door, letting loose a string of obscenities.

Brenda turned in a circle in the cramped quarters, her heart trying to flee her chest. "Go away!" she shouted, realizing the futility of the words after they'd left her mouth. Did she really think he'd shrug and say, *Okie-dokie?*

He pounded and pulled at the door. The tiny building rattled and shook.

Brenda prayed for the latch to hold—there was no place

for her to get a good grip on it—and she was surprised when it *did* hold. She sat on the toilet seat lid and watched the latch closely. "Go away!" she yelled.

The pounding stopped.

Brenda looked up, watching the door. There was the scrape, scrape, scrape of feet on gravel, as if he was pacing back and forth right outside the door.

What was happening? What did he want? She could see the knife so clearly in her mind, the serrations like teeth, ready to bite into her flesh. Was he planning to rape her? Kill her? *Both?*

Christ.

His footsteps stopped. His shadow darkened the glow of the door. He said in a calm tone, "Come out now and I'll make it easy on you. Okay? I won't make you suffer like the others."

The others? Oh, God.

She remembered the red-headed woman. Was she nearby? Maybe she was calling for help at this very moment. Please, please, please let it be so.

"Come on, it'll be quick."

What did he want? Why her? "Go away," Brenda pleaded. She struck the door with the palm of her hand. Waited. Listened. Heard footsteps on gravel pacing back and forth. *I have to outwait him,* she thought. Eventually someone will come along. Someone with a cell phone. What dummy wouldn't have a cell phone on them? *Just a dumb, jogging dummy who's trying to stay in shape for her wedding.*

She'd need to warn them somehow. *The guy waiting next*

to the Biffy Palace has a knife! Call the cops! Hopefully, they wouldn't get close enough to the bastard to get stabbed.

Why didn't I stay home with Mark? He'd been right. Way too hot, way, *way* too hot to be jogging.

In the meantime, she'd wait.

As long as she had to.

I'm not going to die in a Biffy Palace for Christ sake.

If she had to wait for the end of the world, she'd do it. Until then, this outhouse—this damn *Biffy Palace*—was occupied.

There was graffiti on the walls. Phone numbers, epithets, a squirting phallus, an eye with the words *Repent, for the End is Near.* Most was written or drawn in marker, but not the eye—that was *carved* into the fiberglass wall, etched above the toilet paper dispenser with a sharp instrument. And what detail! There was a glint in the eye, the beginning of a tear forming in the corner. The letters below it were written in calligraphy. The time and skill it must have taken to do all that…the *patience.*

Insane patience, Brenda thought. She shivered at the image. Beautiful, but those words…

The End is Near.

Wait, Brenda thought. I should carve my name in the wall. The date, time of day. *Clues,* in case this guy… In case…

And if she *carved* clues in the fiberglass, that guy, that *madman* wouldn't be able to erase it. He could disfigure the writing with his knife, but it would take time, and maybe if she left clues in a few spots, an obvious spot for the killer to see, and then one not so obvious for the cops to find...

Okay, what to write with? Car key! She pulled her Honda key from her pocket and examined it. Normally, she'd have her entire set of keys; house key, car keys for both the Honda and her fiancé's Escape, the key to her parents' house, the key to her office building. But when jogging, all those keys became uncomfortable pressing against her thigh through the thin material of her jogging shorts. She always pared down to the essential Honda key, the rest of the keys waiting for her in the vehicle's glove box.

She hoped that using the key to carve into the Biffy Palace walls wouldn't render it useless. It would suck to race to her car only to find the key no longer worked in the ignition. But she had to take that chance.

Holding the key tightly, she pressed the tip against the hard shell of plastic and began to scratch. It was harder than she'd anticipated. She pressed harder, scratched faster. There. Slowly, but surely, it was working.

BRENDA, she scratched.

Sweat dripped from her face, her neck, adding to the large, growing stain on her tank top.

CHAPMAN.

She tore off lengths of toilet paper, mopped herself off, and dropped the wet paper into the toilet.

952-555-6390.

Her hands and wrists were sore, but she wasn't finished.

Where else? She crouched on one knee and scratched her name and number close to the floor. Her sports bra and tank top felt like a hot, wet sponge. Sweat dripped in her eyes and ears. Jesus, was it hot! And that scent, that cloying scent of vanilla. Only it wasn't really vanilla, was it? No, it was some sort of *faux* vanilla. And that smell barely touched the odor of chemicals and crap coming from the toilet. She reached for another handful of toilet paper, her nose passing within inches of the toilet lid. That shit and chemical smell combined with the faux vanilla…

She gagged.

She needed air, fresh air, otherwise she'd pass out. She stood and leaned her forehead against the wall. The vents near the ceiling weren't helping at all. She stepped onto the toilet and steadied herself with her hands, pressing against opposite walls. She put her face up to one of the vents and took a deep breath.

The air was too still outside.

She'd never thought of herself as claustrophobic before, but here within the protective walls of the Biffy Palace, she found herself longing for wide open spaces, not tiny coffin-like crates made of thick green fiberglass. And it *felt* like a coffin, a puke-green coffin, and she *had* to open the door. Just an inch. Just enough to stick her nose out and take a deep breath of non-vanilla, non-crapchemicalsweat-filled air.

Besides, she hadn't heard a thing outside. Not for quite a while. How long had she been in here?

She stepped quietly off the toilet and listened. No, nothing, unless you counted her increasingly panicked breathing.

She turned the lock on the Biffy Palace door. Pushed it open a crack.

If Brenda had been standing an inch more to the left, the knife blade would've sliced clean through her carotid artery as it sprang through the crack in the door. Instead it merely nicked the side of her neck.

Brenda yanked the door closed on the retreating knife as the killer on the other side tried forcing it back open. Brenda held fast, trying to close the door tight enough to engage the lock, but with the knife held between door and frame, she had no luck. Plus the man on the other side was strong.

God oh God oh God.

"Open the door!"

Oh God oh God.

"C'mon! Open the damn door!"

Maybe that would actually work, Brenda thought. Open the door! She silently counted to three and then shoved outward as hard as she could.

The killer grunted with surprise as he fell backward onto the gravel.

It was all the time Brenda needed to pull the door shut and turn the lock in place.

"It's occupied, fucker!" Brenda screamed.

She heard him scramble in the gravel, heard his footsteps retreat from the Biffy Palace.

Brenda breathed hard. Sweat poured off her in rivers. But she decided then and there that she could take the faux-vanilla scent, the chemically treated smell of shit, the feeling of walls closing in on her. She decided that if today was her day to die, it wouldn't be the goddamn Biffy Palace that did her in.

She waited. Listened. She'd gotten a brief, but better look at the man. After a few minutes she dropped to one knee again and started scratching in the wall.

KILLER--*rest*--CAUCASION--*rest*--BLACK HAIR—*rest*—BIRTHMARK ON—*rest, mop sweat off face and neck*—FOREARM.

What else?

That was enough for now. She got up, stretched as best as she could, pulled down her pants and sat on the toilet. At least here she didn't have to hold anything in.

Half an hour later, she still hadn't heard anything. She grabbed the last of the toilet paper and wiped the sweat from her brow, nose, neck and armpits. She peeled off her tank top, leaving her drenched sports bra in place.

Was it safe, yet?

She was about to stand up on the toilet seat again, this time to try and look out through the vents, but just as she placed one foot up, she heard footsteps.

Were they footsteps? Or was it just the sound of squirrels scurrying in the gravel? She wished the killer would call out to her again. Say something.

She waited. Waited. Imagined Mark in there with her, holding her, heat and claustrophobia be damned! No, wait, she imagined Mark outside, sneaking up on the killer, overtaking him, rescuing her…

The rattling of the door handle snapped her to attention.

She almost said something, but couldn't get the words out. Her throat had grown dry. Occupied, occupied, occupied, she thought to herself frantically, wishing the killer (cause it had to be the killer, right?) got the hint and moved on.

The rattling stopped. Brenda held her breath, listening. There was someone out there, and the silhouette of whoever it was turned the door a darker shade of forest green. Yes, occupied, Brenda thought. Can't you see the little red sign on the door handle? *Occupido,* fucker!

She listened. Pulled in a long, slow breath, quiet as death, and exhaled just as long, slow and quiet. There was a subtle grinding of gravel—shoes sliding across the surface. One step away, two steps. Then—the door handle rattled again, more urgent this time.

Then a voice. "Hey! Is someone in there?" A fist pounded on the door, and Brenda felt as if the fist pounded straight onto her chest.

"Come on lady," came the voice. "My daughter needs to pee!" Then—"Hey, are you okay in there?"

Brenda let out her breath in relief. "Y-yes," she managed. "I'm okay,"

"Well, my little girl here really needs to pee."

Brenda reached for the door, but paused. "Let me hear her," she said.

"What?" The man's voice was agitated.

Was it the same voice she'd heard before? The killer's voice? But this man—his voice wasn't nearly as enraged as the killer's had been.

"What do you mean?" the man asked.

"Can't your daughter say something?"

"Come on, lady, she's gotta go. Bad!"

Brenda studied the silhouette. It was distorted, too

distorted to tell if there really were two people out there, father and daughter. She leaned her head against the door, listening, sweat dripping off nose, chin, and neck.

More pounding on the door. "Come on, lady!"

"Make your daughter say something," Brenda pleaded. She wanted to be sure. She changed tactics. "There's a killer out there," she said.

"What?"

"A killer! I saw him. Call 911. Get the police. Just get out of here!"

"There's no one out here, lady. Just me and my daughter, and she's gonna mess her pants if—"

"I need to hear her voice! Do you understand?"

"Come on, you're making her cry. You sick—where do you get off scaring a kid?"

"There's a killer out there!"

"Open up the damn door!" His voice softened. "It's okay, honey. There's no killer here. Can't you just go in the grass? Come on, sweety."

Damn it, damn it, damn it. Brenda relented. "Okay, okay," she said. She turned the door handle. Pushed the door open a crack. Saw the back of a man leaning over, hovering over his daughter, his body blocking Brenda's view.

"Come on, honey, she's coming out now. Stop crying, okay?"

"Here," Brenda said. "I'm coming out, okay? The bathroom's all yours. Okay?"

She pushed the door all the way open. The man spun around.

Of course there was no little girl, no daughter. Brenda only saw a flash of steel, one big nasty hunting knife, and there was blood on it, and for a fraction of a second she saw a bit of flesh hanging off the serrated edge. He lunged at her.

But not fast enough.

Brenda dove back into the Biffy Palace, back to her sanctuary just in time, slamming the door shut as the knife's tip collided with the hardened forest green fiberglass.

"Fuck!" the killer cried. "Fuck, fuck, fuck!"

At least the brief burst of fresh air diluted the smell of vanilla, the smell of chemicals and feces. Brenda wondered if she'd ever get that scent out of her nose. *If I survive.* It seemed like the smell was embedded deep up her nostrils, clinging to her nasal cavity, and if she could reach up inside her nose and claw that smell out—*if I survive*—she wouldn't hesitate.

The man—the killer—stopped yelling. Brenda could almost feel him collecting himself, plotting, thinking. Okay, *you* gotta think, Brenda thought. He knows I'm in here. I should've stayed silent.

There was her key. The hand sanitizer dispenser. Okay, okay. The toilet seat cover, the toilet paper dispenser. Possible weapons? She wiggled the plastic seat from side to side. *Can I yank it off?* Maybe use it as a shield, and the sanitizer dispenser could be a clubbing device. *Or my key*—if I could just fend off the first thrust of his knife with the toilet seat lid, then I could drive my key into one of his eyes.

He's not going to just let me go, is he? she thought.

What else could she do? She listened. Heard the man's shoes on the gravel. Walking this way and that. The glow in the Biffy Palace grew muted.

The sun's going down, she realized. *How long have I been in here?*

She glanced down into the toilet. Wished it led to a series of tunnels. If she could get down there, then maybe she could escape. But no—this was a modern outhouse, a goddamn Biffy Palace! She'd seen the trucks rolling down the highway. Biffy Palace! We're Number 1 at Dealing with Number 2! They had big hoses that sucked the waste right out from the large storage containers nestled beneath the toilets. That's how they did it nowadays. No mere big hole (complete with escape tunnels!) dug into the ground. Besides, who was she kidding? She couldn't fit through that toilet hole even if she wanted to. At best, she'd get stuck at the hips, and then what good could she do?

Okay. Think.

Toilet seat lid shield. Honda key. Open the door expecting the lunge. Side-step it and block with the shield, then ram the key home. Bury it deep into his eye socket.

The car key was thick and long. Who cared if she couldn't start the car as long as the killer was incapacitated?

So—drive the key into his eye, then take away his knife, and then—

—and then do what you have to do.

She realized the crunch of shoes on gravel had stopped. She listened. She couldn't hear anything. The light from the outside continued to dim. *Get the toilet seat lid off.* She lifted it open and kicked out at it with her right foot. It merely bent back an inch until it touched the back wall. Simply kicking it off wouldn't work.

She listened some more.

Nothing.

She kneeled onto the floor and examined the lid's hinge, trying her best to ignore the smells wafting from below. She no longer tried to stem the flow of sweat pouring off of her. She was, however, very thirsty. She knew she was in serious need of water, but for now she had to concentrate on the task at hand.

Okay, a hinge. A hinge. She didn't see any screws to unscrew. Just…a plastic hinge.

She grit her teeth and grabbed both sides of the lid. She yanked it from side to side. *Let loose, you bastard!* She stood and leaned over it, trying to twist it. *Come on, come on.* She grunted. *Not giving.* She positioned herself to one side and put both hands on the opposite side of the lid and pulled it toward her hard. *Yank, yank.*

There! Something gave. It started to loosen.

Yank, yank, yank.

Damn it. She paused to catch her breath, and then pulled again. *Yank.* Finally! It came free. She sat down on the horse-shoe shaped toilet seat, panting. The sunlight was quickly fading.

She needed to rest. Her arms ached. Cramps wracked her body. There wasn't enough room to properly stretch. *Why won't he just go away?*

There was the sudden sound of liquid splattering against the wall. She sat up straight, listening. Is he peeing? Sounded like it. The killer began to walk around the outhouse, pissing against the walls. For a brief moment, she wondered if he was marking his territory.

But, no. It wasn't pee. Above the smell of faux vanilla and chemicals and shit, she smelled lighter fluid.

Lighter fluid. I*s he going to burn me alive? Inside the Biffy Palace?* And her message, her painstakingly carved message— *both* messages—were going to simply melt away.

He wants me to come running out. That's what he's expecting.

Sure enough, she heard the strike of a lighter, followed by the *whoosh* of igniting lighter fluid. She watched the flickering glow from the flames grow outside the outhouse. Noxious, black smoke crept through the vents in thickening tendrils. Brenda began to blink as the fumes brought stinging tears to her eyes.

She had to act. Act fast before the smoke overcame her. She clutched her key between her index and middle fingers and held the toilet seat lid over her head.

She felt light-headed. No time for prayer. No time for one last reflection over her life. *It's now or never.*

I'm a goddamn warrior princess, she thought as she undid the latch and kicked the door open. She let out a war cry and ducked as a knife flashed above her head. She blindly struck out with her key and felt it strike flesh.

"Bitch!" the killer screamed.

Bull's-eye.

She ran and felt the knife's blade catch her shoulder. She spun and swung the toilet lid hard at the killer's hand. Another bull's-eye and the knife flew through the air. The killer reached out for her, his cheek bleeding from the slash of her key. She swung the toilet lid again, this time connecting with the side of his face. She kicked out her leg and tripped him. He stumbled and fell to his knees.

Brenda only now started to feel the pain of the cut on her shoulder, but she lifted the plastic lid and brought it down on top of the killer's head. Once. Twice. *Three times a lady,* she thought, the third swing connecting with his nose, sending blood spraying. The killer fell onto his side and weakly held up a hand in surrender.

Brenda swung at his hand and felt the give of his breaking fingers.

She held the seat above her for another swing, breathing hard.

A woman called out from beyond her range of vision. "Hey!"

Brenda looked up. *Oh dear sweet Jesus, thank you, thank you, thank you.* It was the redheaded woman.

"A phone," Brenda gasped. "Do you have a phone?"

"Yes. Yes, back at my campsite. What's going on?"

"This—this *man*—attacked me. Tried to kill me. Please, call the police. An ambulance."

"Yes. God. Okay. Come with me."

"But—" Brenda indicated the man lying on the ground at her feet. He was still breathing.

"He doesn't look like he's in any shape to do much harm now," the woman said. "Come on. It'll be okay. Besides—" She bent down and picked up the killer's knife. "We have this. You want it?"

She wanted nothing to do with it. How many others had it killed? "God, no," Brenda said.

The redhead smiled slightly. "You look like you can handle a toilet seat with the best of them."

"Yes," Brenda breathed. "I'm a goddamn warrior princess." She noticed that the lighter fluid had burned itself out.

The redhead put an arm around Brenda's shoulders. "Come on. The campsite's not far."

Brenda shuddered with relief. She slumped against the redhead's side.

The sound of something scraping on gravel behind them made her spin around. The killer slowly rose to his knees. "Celia," he groaned.

Celia?

Brenda jumped aside just as the redhead *(Celia?)* thrust the knife at her. She fell to the ground and rolled quickly toward the toiled lit, grabbed it and sprang up, blocking another swing of the knife just in time.

Brenda screamed with rage and swung the Honda key at the (Celia?) redhead. This time she did not swing blindly, and she plunged the key straight into Celia's left eye, all the way up to her knuckles.

Celia, that goddamn redhead, screamed in pain. Brenda grabbed the knife from her and kicked her hard in the shin. There was the sickening sound of cracking bone. Celia fell to her side, writhing and clutching at the hole where her eye had been.

"Celia," the man grunted.

Brenda turned toward him.

He kneeled in the gravel, his face bruised and bleeding, his eyes straining to fully open.

"You are pitiful," Brenda whispered. She raised the knife above her head. "And I am a goddamn warrior *queen.*"

White Crosses

They drove the Blue Goose up US Highway 191 from the town of West Yellowstone toward their campsite some forty miles north near Big Sky, Montana. Noah Johnson, a fresh inductee of the octogenarian club, sat somewhat hunched behind the wheel, while Dick Varney, seventy-nine, rode shotgun, his forehead against the window, hardly noticing the lush scenery of the Gallatins.

Twenty-four, he counted. *Twenty-five, twenty-six.*

The Blue Goose had served as a school bus in Brainerd, but Varney and Johnson bought it at auction, gutted it, and added a few luxuries—cupboards, beds, a table, chairs—converting it into an RV of sorts. They painted it blue and along each side wrote the words *Blue Goose,* as if it were a boat. And it was a boat of sorts, but instead of carrying them over lakes and seas, it drove them over the winding roads crisscrossing the country.

"Twenty-seven," Varney counted, now out loud. "Twenty-eight."

"You say something?" Johnson asked.

"I've counted twenty-eight so far." Varney pointed out the window. "Twenty-nine. Thirty."

"Don't do that," Johnson said.

"There's a few more every year."

Traffic fatalities, marked by white crosses to remind drivers to slow down on the winding canyon roads nestled within the Gallatins.

Dick and Noah ran the Arrow Point Resort, a small operation back in Minnesota, half-an-hour north of Brainerd, renting out cabins, a few boats; they sold gas to boats from the other properties situated on the shores of interconnecting lakes. But they closed the place for the last couple weeks of September as they had for the last eleven years to drive out to Yellowstone; to sight-see, fish, catch up on reading, and visit the place where Kimberly died. Kimberly and the rest of her family; husband Jack, daughter Jill, son Benjamin.

They pulled the Blue Goose into the Swan Creek Campground, got out, stretched, rigged up a makeshift awning on the side of the bus, and set up two collapsible camping chairs. Most of that day had been spent in Yellowstone, Varney fishing and Johnson sitting on the bank reading John D. MacDonald novels.

The campground was small, only a dozen or so sites, and only half were occupied. It was late September and the Gallatin River rushed past, cool and rippling with trout. Varney piled kindling and sticks into a mound in their fire ring while Johnson gave him unnecessary pointers from his chair. Finally, with the fire going, Varney stood. "You gonna just sit there, or help me out?"

Johnson sighed and lifted himself out of his camping chair. "Hold on, I'm coming." He was lean and wiry, but lately had taken to tiring easily, and out here in the mountains, he needed another couple of days to acclimate to the altitude.

They wandered beneath lodge pole pines looking for a few good fallen branches. It didn't take long. They carried them back and set them between their chairs. Varney set to whittling while Johnson dove back into his book.

A pickup truck with a small camper rumbled into the empty site next to them, gravel popping beneath its tires. A man got out from behind the wheel in a faded red tank top, cut-off shorts and flip-flops. A girl emerged yawning from the passenger side, her brown hair cut short. Varney figured she couldn't be more than twelve or thirteen, although he'd long ago given up believing he could predict someone's age with any accuracy.

They watched the newcomers for a moment before going back to their respective pursuits of reading and whittling. The shade of the mountains soon turned to the genuine darkness of night, and Varney, satisfied with his progress on the branches, took the two trout he'd caught that morning in Yellowstone out of the cooler. He carried the fish down to the river and squatted at its edge. He grabbed a chilled trout by the lower jaw and yanked until the whole belly tore off with it, the entrails spilling into the swift current. He rinsed the fish in the cold river, repeated the procedure with the second one, and carried them dripping back to the Blue Goose. After cooking them over the fire in a pan of hot oil, Varney salted them and eased them onto paper plates.

"Mind the bones," he warned, as he and Johnson sat at the picnic table, the glow of fire casting its orange light on them.

The scent of a cigarette drifted over from nearby.

Varney looked toward the newcomers' camper from which the young girl had emerged earlier. It was dark, save for the glowing tip of cigarette. "What the hell?" Varney mumbled. "No campfire? No roasted marshmallows for the girl?"

"Invite 'em over," Johnson said. "We've got plenty of fixins for s'mores."

Varney studied the camper and said in a low voice, "Something doesn't seem right about that situation."

Johnson chuckled. "A father and daughter on a trip? Like how you took Kimberly on that trip to the Black Hills? The Grand Canyon? Yellowstone?"

Varney stopped him from going on. "This is different."

"Mind your own business, Dick," Johnson warned.

Varney set his jaw. "I'll invite them over. Like you said, we got plenty of fixins." He wiped his hands off on his jeans and walked toward the dark trailer, stepping carefully. Last thing he needed was another sprained ankle. Johnson broke his toe earlier that summer tripping over an exposed root back at the resort, and it took a helluva long time to heal.

Varney neared the glowing cigarette tip and made out a silhouette to go with it—a man in a lawn chair.

Varney stopped. "Hello," he said.

The man grunted. "Hey."

"Your daughter asleep?" Varney asked.

The man took a drag off of his cigarette and tipped back a beer. He looked up at Varney. "Why?"

Varney shrugged in the darkness. "My friend and I thought she might like to join us by the fire and roast a few marshmallows. You're welcome, too, of course. We have all the fixins for s'mores."

Another drag of cigarette. "She's asleep."

A voice came from the camper; "Who're you talking to, Jim?"

"No one," Jim called before guiding the cigarette back to his mouth.

"It'd be no trouble," Varney said.

"Thanks," Jim said. "But no."

"Okay," Varney said, then mumbled, "Sorry I asked." He stepped carefully back to the light of the fire and the familiar shape of the Blue Goose.

"Well?" Johnson asked as Varney settled in next to him at the fire.

Varney raised his eyebrows. "Not very social." He kept his voice low. "That poor girl. I think she got dealt a piss-poor hand for a father. She didn't even call him *Dad.*"

"Maybe it's not her father. Maybe it's an uncle. Or a new step-dad."

They watched the fire. Varney shook his head. "Something just ain't right about that situation." He pulled a beer from a small cooler and cracked it open, then twisted the cap off of a single-serve bottle of Chardonnay and handed it to Johnson. They raised their beverages to the fire. "Here's to Kimmy," Varney said.

"To Kimmy," Johnson said, the fading SEMPER FI tattoo on his left bicep flexing.

They both sipped and watched the flames and the undulating glow of the hot coals.

An hour later, as Varney sat with his arm around Johnson, footsteps crunched the gravel. Varney withdrew his arm.

"Hi!" It was the girl from the camper.

Varney stood. "Why hello there. You decided to join us after all."

"I'm Noah," Johnson said, reaching out to shake the girl's hand.

The girl grinned in the firelight, grabbed Johnson's hand and pumped it up and down. "Kelly," she said. She looked at Varney. "Got any marshmallows left?"

"Sure," Varney said. He fetched the bag and a roasting stick from the picnic table. "Help yourself."

"We got fixins for s'mores," Johnson said.

"Is your dad going to join us?" Varney asked.

Kelly skewered two marshmallows onto the end of her stick and maneuvered them over the coals. "He's not my dad," she said. "Besides, he's passed out."

"Oh," Johnson said.

Varney felt something rise in his throat, but he tamped it down.

"You help yourself to as many marshmallows as you want," Johnson said.

"He an uncle?" Varney asked.

The marshmallows caught fire and Kelly pulled them from the flame and blew them out. "No. That's Jim. He's a friend of my dad's. He's bringing me out to visit him."

"Ah," Varney said. "Your folks divorced, I take it?"

"They weren't ever married. I've only seen pictures of my dad."

"But you're going to visit him?"

"Yep."

Varney glanced at Johnson, then back to the girl. He slowly asked, "And your mom…she knows about this, right?"

"Course she knows." Kelly looked incredulously at Varney.

Johnson cleared his throat. "Is Jim a nice man?"

Kelly popped a burnt marshmallow into her mouth. "I guess," she said, talking around it. "He doesn't talk much." She swallowed. "But he lets me play his Game Boy."

"Game Boy?" Johnson asked.

"Yeah. You know—a Nintendo?"

Varney said to Johnson, "It's one of those computer things." He turned to Kelly. "We've got a phone in the bus if you want to call your mom."

"Really?"

"You know her number?"

"Of course I know her number. It's just that Jim said I shouldn't call her because she's so busy with work."

Johnson leaned forward. "I'm sure it will be fine this one time. Besides, it's late, and I'd bet anything she'd love to hear your voice."

"I'll go get the phone," Varney said. He jogged to the Goose. Inside, he searched for the cell phone. It wasn't something they used much; it was there for emergencies and not much else.

Was *this* an emergency?

If the girl calls her mother and everything is hunky dory, Varney thought, than it will at least put *my* mind at ease.

There. Next to the sink. He checked to make sure it was charged. Good to go.

He walked back to the campfire and held the phone out to Kelly. "You want me to dial?"

Kelly took it from Varney. "I know how to use a phone."

As she started to tap in the numbers, there was the sound of crunching debris again.

Jim.

"There you are. What do you think you're doing?"

Before Kelly could answer, Varney said, "She's calling her mother." He turned to the girl. "Go ahead, honey."

Jim grabbed the phone and tossed it back to Varney. "It's past her bedtime."

Varney took a step forward. Johnson tensed next to him. "Let her call home. Just to say goodnight to her mother." He held the phone out to Kelly.

Kelly looked at Jim.

"Her mom is asleep," Jim said, emphasizing each word.

"I doubt she'd mind a quick call from her daughter," Varney said.

"She can call her tomorrow," Jim said. "When she's awake."

"Do you want to call your mom," Varney asked Kelly.

"*Varney,*" Johnson warned.

"Here," Jim said, taking the phone out of Varney's hand.

He turned to Kelly. "What's your mom's number?"

Kelly recited the numbers. Varney thought he heard a slight tremor in her voice, but there was the sound of the river and the wind rustling the pine trees, so he couldn't be sure.

Jim dialed the phone and held it to his ear. After a moment he shook his head. "She ain't answering."

"Let me try," Varney said.

Jim snorted. "Come on, Kelly. It's way past your bedtime." He tossed the phone back to Varney and grabbed Kelly's hand.

Varney fumbled with the phone, almost dropping it into the fire. "Wait," he said.

"Varney." Johnson grabbed his elbow.

"Thanks for the marshmallows," Kelly said. She and Jim disappeared into the darkness.

Varney whispered harshly, "See? I told you something was off about them. I'm calling the police."

"Varney, *no.*"

"She's being kidnapped."

"You don't know that."

"You don't think there's something strange going on?"

Johnson sipped his Chardonnay. "I don't know. I don't think he's hurting her, if that's what you mean. The man is drunk, but the girl seems okay."

"But *kidnapping?*"

"That's a leap."

"Why wouldn't he let her call her mother?"

"You heard what he said. And he *did* try," Johnson said.

"Remember?"

"Did he? Do you think he actually dialed the number?"

"Isn't there a way to check?" Johnson asked.

Varney held the phone up and examined it. "Ah," he said. It showed the last number dialed. He held it out to show Johnson. "Was this it?"

Johnson squinted at it. "The area code seems familiar. Why don't you call it?"

Varney carefully touched the number on the smart phone's screen and held the device up to his ear. A moment later he frowned.

"What?" Johnson asked.

"The number's been disconnected," Varney said.

Johnson looked beyond Varney to the Blue Goose. "Maybe he misdialed," he said softly. "He was drunk."

Varney stared at Johnson, contemplating his partner of thirty-three years. Johnson was a good man. Ex-marine (although once a marine, always a marine, Johnson always reminded him). Kids and grandkids of his own.

Why can't he see what's going on. Varney was about to vent his frustration, but Johnson sighed, placed a hand on the small of his back and rubbed. "Call the police," Johnson said. "Ask if there are any missing children named Kelly."

Varney looked at Johnson, then at the sparks of the campfire floating toward the sky. He breathed in the cool, intoxicating mountain air. It had been him, Varney, who had first shown Kimberly the beauty of this area when she was fourteen, and *she* had fallen in love with the area as much as *he* had so many years before. She brought her own family out here in their mini-van how many times? Before…

It was so hard to think about, even after a decade had passed. Kimberly was the one perfect thing he had ever created. She was—*still* was—the love of his life.

Kimmy.

Damn it.

Tears blurred his eyes.

Johnson continued rubbing his back. "Let's go to bed," he said quietly. "They'll be here in the morning. Especially in his condition."

Varney came back to the present and wiped his eyes with his jacket sleeve. "He better not even think of driving before he's sobered up." Then he said, "You go on to bed. I'm gonna stay up for a little while."

"You sure?" Johnson asked.

Varney nodded and picked up the branches he'd been working on earlier. Johnson shambled back to the Blue Goose. There was the sound of the river and the wind in the pines. There was the sound of the campfire and the sound of Varney's pocketknife shaving off thin strips of wood from the branches gathered earlier.

When Varney woke the next morning, the air was somewhere south of fifty-degrees. *Chilly.* Johnson heated a pot of coffee and cooked eggs and bacon on their Coleman stove.

"That smell never gets old," Varney said, stepping behind Johnson.

"You're lucky," Johnson said. "My sniffer hasn't worked

worth a crap for I don't know how long."

"Maybe *you're* the lucky one," Varney said and farted.

"Classy." Johnson dished up plates of bacon and eggs and poured two cups of coffee; Varney's with two sugars and cream, Johnson's black. They took their breakfast out to the picnic table and sat shivering and eating and watching the smoke rise from beneath the layer of dirty-white ash that remained in the fire ring.

Varney lifted a forkful of eggs to his mouth, but stopped halfway. He looked over at the pick-up and camper across from them. He'd forgotten about them this morning, about Kelly and that drunkard Jim until just this moment. God, how his mind worked these days…

He asked Johnson, "Notice anything going on over there?"

"Nope," Johnson said. "Quiet as a kitten."

"Must still be asleep." Varney stared at the camper. In the morning light, everything about it seemed a lot less sinister. He shook his head, decided to wait until Kelly was awake and Jim was sober. Try talking to them a little more. If he still had a bad feeling about the whole thing, he'd put in a call to the police. Besides, he had the truck's license plate number already written down on the back of an envelope, along with a description of the vehicle and camper, of Kelly and Jim. He didn't want to trust his memory to something like this.

Johnson cleaned up after breakfast and got out a book while Varney ambled down to the river, an empty five-gallon bucket in hand. He meant to fill it and pour the water over the still active coals before they left. He kneeled carefully at the river's edge and pushed the bucket under the strong, cold water. It filled immediately. As he hefted it back up onto shore, he saw something move out of the corner of his eye. He squinted. Sitting about thirty feet downriver was that girl, Kelly. Shivering.

Varney set the heavy bucket down and walked carefully along the uneven riverbank. Kelly didn't look up until he stood directly over her. Her eyes were bloodshot, the skin beneath them dark and puffy. She'd been crying.

Varney kneeled next to her. "Honey, what's the matter? Are you okay?"

She nodded at first, but the nod turned to a head shake; a reluctant no.

Varney took off his quilted flannel jacket and wrapped it around her. "You're freezing. Are you hurt?"

She smiled pathetically, the smile of a young girl trying to put on a brave face, but the smile dissolved into tears. She shook her head weakly, unconvincingly.

Varney grimaced. "Did that man do something to you?" Anger rose in the deepest part of his gut. He grew hot.

Kelly didn't answer, didn't nod or shake her head. Instead, she stared at the river, her shivering constant.

"Come on," Varney said, standing. "Come with me."

Kelly stayed put.

"I've got a phone, remember? We'll call the police. You can call your mother."

When she still wouldn't stand, Varney looked around him. Seeing no one else near, he said, "Okay, stay put. I'll be back in a moment." He paused. "You understand?"

Again, no response. When Varney got back to the campsite, he said to Johnson, "Goddamn it, get the phone."

"Why?"

"I shouldn't have let you talk me out of—" He stopped before he said something he'd regret later. "Get the gun."

"What's going—"

"Just get it!" Varney snapped. He stomped over to the camper, not waiting for Johnson, and swung the flimsy door open. "Where the hell are you?" he shouted. "What the hell did you do to her?"

There was no answer.

But there was something, a shape filling a green sleeping bag on one of the bunks. Varney stared at it. *Jesus, he's still sleeping?*

Varney strode over to the sleeping bag and shook it.

Johnson flung open the camper's door and jogged up the few steps carrying their shotgun. "Are you crazy?" he shouted. "Are you trying to get yourself killed?"

Varney ignored his partner. Instead, he peeled back the sleeping bag. A strange look came over his face. "Oh," he said.

"What?" Johnson asked.

Varney stepped aside. They both looked at the man lying there. Jim.

A quiet voice from the doorway startled them. "I did it," Kelly said. "I killed him." She ran to Varney and threw her arms around him, sobbing.

They walked her over to the Blue Goose. Warmed up a mug of hot chocolate. Johnson topped it with a couple of marshmallows while Kelly waited on a small cushioned bench at the narrow table where the two men often played Rummy.

"What should we do?" Varney asked Johnson, keeping his voice low as they sat next to each other on their bed.

"What do you mean? Isn't it obvious?"

Varney shook his head. "No. It's not."

"We call the police. We should've already called them by now."

"But she did it in self-defense."

Johnson nodded. "Of course. And the police will sort all that out."

"What if they don't, and—"

"She's a minor," Johnson interrupted.

Varney looked over at her. "She's so young. The moment we call the police, her childhood will be over."

Johnson put an arm around Varney and pulled him close. "Her life changed the moment that man took her from her mother. And her childhood won't be over. Like you said, it was self-defense. Things will be crazy for a while, sure, but life will go on." He hugged Varney. "Kids are tough. You know that."

"But…" Varney shook his head.

"What?"

Varney looked pleadingly into Johnson's eyes. "You *know* what day it is."

"Oh," Johnson said. "I see." Then he said, "But after…"

"What if I tell the police *I* did it? *I* killed the man."

Johnson let go of Varney. "Are you nuts?"

Tears welled up in Varney's eyes. He sobbed as Johnson hugged him tightly and rocked with him back and forth on the edge of the bed. "It's just...I just..." Varney tried to choke back the tears.

Kelly walked over to them. "I'm sorry I made you cry, mister," she said.

Varney looked up at her. "No, no. It's not about that." He swallowed. "Honey, you've got to know you didn't do anything wrong."

"Then why are you crying?"

They poured the bucket of water over the coals in the fire pit, cleaned up their site and packed up the Blue Goose. Johnson drove. Varney sat at the Rummy table next to Kelly. "I had a little girl," he said. "You remind me of her. She grew up and had a family. Two kids." Tears flowed over his cheeks. Every once in a while Johnson glanced up at him in the rearview mirror, concern reflected in his eyes.

"I think she was happy," Varney said. "In fact, I know she was happy, despite the problems her mother and I had."

"Where is she now?"

Varney looked out the window. "See those white crosses we pass by every so often?"

Kelly nodded. She asked softly, "Did she die out here?"

Varney smiled as best he could, but could no longer talk.

The bus soon slowed and pulled over onto a gravel shoulder. Johnson parked and they all got out, watching and listening carefully for oncoming traffic. It was a narrow spot in the canyon, metal guardrails next to a drop-off to the river on one side, the steep rock face of mountain on the other. And in between wound the road with only a narrow gravel shoulder.

Johnson asked Varney, "You okay to do this?"

Varney shrugged.

Kelly walked between the two men over to the four metal crosses painted white and bunched together like a bouquet. Varney carried his own crosses, the ones he'd whittled and decorated in his own way the night before Kelly killed Jim. Johnson carried a hard, rubber mallet.

Johnson held each of the wooden crosses as Varney pounded them in next to the impersonal metal ones. Then Varney went back to the Blue Goose and came outside with four stuffed animals. He placed them at the feet of the makeshift crosses.

Johnson took Kelly by the hand and led her back to the bus. "Let's leave him alone for a bit."

They sat in the bus while Varney knelt on the spot his daughter, grand-kids and son-in-law had died over a decade ago. Finally, he stood and touched each of the handmade crosses, turned and walked back to the Blue Goose.

As he climbed the steps, he said, "I don't think I can come out here again. It's too hard, and I'm too old." It was the same thing he said every year. He sat next to Kelly. Smiled at her. "You've got a lot of years ahead of you. You know that, don't you? Things will work out," he said. "It'll turn out okay."

He hoped it was true.

Johnson pulled cautiously away from the shoulder and

back onto US Highway 191, headed back to the Swan Creek Campground. They drove past more of the stark, white crosses amidst the lulling beauty and seductive grandeur of the mountains, the canyons, and the swiftly flowing rivers.

Varney turned on his phone and called the police.

Mississippi Pearl

Some of you might remember my sister, Kelly Holmsted. At fourteen, she made the papers when she pried open an American pearly freshwater mussel from Lake Pepin and pulled out a perfect white sphere nearly the size of a cherry; the largest Mississippi pearl ever found. A dealer offered her five thousand dollars for it, but she refused. He offered seven thousand, and again, she refused.

"Think of the tuition it would cover," our father said.

"You can save it for your wedding," Mom said. "Think of the honeymoon you could have. You could *fly* somewhere."

I was only eight at the time, and the answer seemed simple. "I've got marbles bigger than that," I said. "Take the money."

But Kelly wouldn't part with it. She brushed a lock of light auburn hair from her eyes. "How can I sell something so beautiful? So perfect?"

She kept the pearl secure in a small black velvet pouch attached to a silver necklace Mom had given her for her thirteenth birthday. Although the chain never left her neck, she often lifted the pouch from her deepening cleavage and carefully plucked the pearl from its folds to feel the cool, smooth hardness in the palm of her hand. She'd stare at it, mouth slightly parted, eyes filled with the pearl's reflection. I'd have to shout to get her attention.

She let me hold it only once, watching my every move, as if I might try to steal it if she so much as blinked. I tossed it in the air just to see how it felt to catch something so valuable.

She nearly choked on her own gasp. "You're done," she said and pried the pearl from my sweaty palm.

But as careful as she was, vigilant to a fault, she lost it only five weeks later.

She stood outside the screen door crying, both hands pressed against the wire mesh, her khaki shorts and white blouse muddied and soaked with rain. Several of her fingernails were broken, and her forearms and knees were scraped and bleeding. "It's gone," she said through the screen.

Mom hesitated only a moment, looking her daughter over and swallowing back a look of anguish that frightened me. She yanked open the door and took Kelly's hand. "Oh, honey—what happened?"

My big sister didn't seem so big anymore as she stepped across the threshold and collapsed into Mom's arms. Dad and I watched stupidly while she bawled, until Mom finally coaxed her into the bathroom and shut the door. Running bath water muffled any words that were said.

Later, this is what Mom told me;

Kelly dropped the pearl while walking home. A rush of rainwater swept it into the gutter and washed it down a storm-drain. Kelly bloodied her skin by lying on gravel and broken glass trying to reach through the rusty grate for it. *And she's very upset about it, Michael, so don't you dare bring it up to her. Understand?*

I nodded. I'd wanted to ask about the small bruises on Kelly's neck, but Mom's eyes insisted that the subject was closed.

And it was.

But that was over thirty years ago.

It's early March and I'm ready for winter to be over, especially after the white-knuckle drive to my parents' new house on Lake Krenshaw. I'm surprised at how big the place is, surprised they could afford a lake home like this, but I guess that's what you get for being thrifty your whole life. My wife Corinne and daughter Amanda are home with the flu, and a big part of me wishes I stayed with them. But Kelly's visiting from Nebraska, and it's rare that I get to see her.

Mom's got peppermint tea on. Dad and I munch on homemade chocolate chip cookies. Kelly's husband Bruce stands at the bay window scratching his neck and draining a glass of bourbon.

"Nice view," he says, staring at the snow swirling in the darkness.

His sarcasm grows more pronounced with each drink that slides past his well-oiled tongue. I've only been here thirty minutes, and I'm already sick to death of him. But instead of giving into the urge to tell him to shut the hell up, I ignore him and divert my parents' attention.

"Am I crazy, or does anyone else recall a junked up Cadillac sitting out on Lake Pepin when I was a kid? Folks took bets on when it would fall through the ice?"

"You're crazy," Dad says around a mouthful of cookie.

"I remember that," says Mom. "You'd buy a ticket and write down the date and time you thought it would fall through the ice. Sure I remember that."

"You think a car could still drive out there?" Kelly asks.

Bruce grimaces. "Are you nuts? You'd fall through in a second." He swirls the melting ice in his glass. "I could use another drink, Kel."

Her shaking is worse than ever. It's mainly her head, and we'd feared Parkinson's, but her doctor insists it's just stress.

She starts to stand, but I wave her down. "I'll get it." I pour his drink and set it on the table with a loud thunk.

Stress.

"Russian Park," Dad says.

My mind back-pedals. "What?"

"That's where they put the cars in at. Russian Park. Drained the oil and gas so they wouldn't leak. Attached a chain to the axle so once they broke through they could winch them back in."

Cars on the ice. Back to that again.

"They stopped doing it once kids started spray-painting cuss words on the exterior. Ken Olson said they found used condoms in the seats. Remember Ken Olson?" he asks.

Mom nods. Her and Dad's hair have turned the same shade of silver, and it's already hard to remember it any other way.

Bruce finishes his drink with a loud slurp and comes back for another.

When I arrived that day, the ice out on Lake Krenshaw looked rippled and distressed. The fishing shanties had been hauled off, except for one that broke through two weeks ago and refroze half in and half out of the lake.

"I bet you could drive out there," Kelly says. "As cold as it's been lately."

"Take the goddamn truck out there and try it, then," Bruce says. "But when you break through the ice, I'm going after the truck before I try saving your sorry ass."

"*Bruce,*" Kelly says. It's just the one word, but we all catch the inflection she gives it.

Bruce's eyes harden. He's a piece of work, all right; a blustering, unkempt, alcohol slurping piece of work. "What?"

Kelly ignores him. The shaking of her head seems like an attempt to hold in her anger.

But Bruce won't let it go. His lips twitch. "What?"

Kelly nods at his drink. "Take it easy."

He grunts and pours himself another.

The intensity of Dad's breathing increases through his nose. Mom searches the cupboard and pulls down a container of Tylenol, pops two in her mouth and follows it with a swig of tea.

"Enough, already," Kelly says.

"Enough what?"

All five-foot-three of Kelly stands and grabs the drink from his hand. She dumps the contents into the sink. "Stop embarrassing me."

Bruce grabs another glass, slams it on the counter and fills it to the top. *"Me* embarrass *you?"*

Funny thing is, now I want a stiff drink. I want to numb the shit I'm hearing. I want to make it easier to deal with this *stress.*

Huh—stress.

Listen, stress is driving behind a semi spewing slush on your windshield. Stress is your baby burning with fever. What makes Kelly's head shake, *doctor,* isn't stress.

"Bruce," Kelly says.

"What?"

How many times have I imagined my arm uncoiling like a snake, my fist connecting with the bridge of Bruce's nose, the feel of his cartilage and bone crumbling beneath my knuckles?

"Bruce!"

How many times?

But tonight, *his* hand flies out. Connects with Kelly's cheek and nose. Makes a sound so awful, the sound of skin hitting skin, and damn it, I could sure use a drink, I could sure use permission to cover my ears, close my eyes and chant "nah nah nah" loud enough to take away that sound, that sickening sound that no one should ever have to hear.

Kelly's face turns bright red. Blood trickles from her nose. Her eyes grow wide and wet.

The rage, the anger I feel, immobilizes me. I look at my mother. My father. Mom's frozen, too. Dad says, "Hey," and starts to stand, but he stops. Frozen. It's so foreign to us. So unreal. See, this isn't our world, this isn't our life.

We sit and watch like deer caught in headlights. Why can't I speak? Why can't I do something?

Then Mom, God bless her, rolls her shoulders back, sears Bruce with her eyes, and says, "We do not hit in this house." In her voice are forty-some years of teaching crowded elementary school classrooms.

Bruce grunts, grabs a pack of Camels off the kitchen counter and walks out the front door into the cold, slamming the door behind him. We let out a collective breath.

Stress, huh?

Mom wets a washcloth and hands it to Kelly. Dad drops onto the sofa. His eyes find refuge in a basketball game. Kelly wipes the blood off her nose and tears from the corners of her eyes. Mom takes the washcloth from her and rinses it out in the sink. I wonder if Dad sees the game, or does he still see Bruce's hand striking his daughter?

"C'mon, Kel," I finally say. "Let's go watch the snow."

I take her hand and lead her out to the screened-in porch beneath the deck out back. Wicker furniture stands covered and stacked against the walls. Cold wind blows through the screens and stirs up the smell of freshly stained wood. I feel light-headed and hollow. "How often does he hit you?" I ask.

Her trembling stops for a moment. Her eyes fix on the lake, on the dark pools of water forming on top of the ice. "He's slapped me a few times," she says. "When I've done something dumb."

I stare at her. Crumble inside as her head starts shaking again. "God, Kelly. You're not dumb."

She wipes at her eyes with the heel of her hand. "Gotta

be dumb to still be with him, don't I?"

"You can't live like this." The words come out in ragged syllables, and I almost choke on them. "You've got to leave him."

The snow and wind stops as if someone's flipped a switch and the moon appears as a dirty talc haze behind emaciated clouds.

Kelly's cheeks are streaked with the trails of hot tears.

"Kelly? Look at me."

She looks, her lips pressed tightly together, breath forced slowly in and out through her nose. Then she looks out at the lake. I follow her eyes. The ice is covered with dirty slush and deepening pools of black water.

I put my hand on her shoulder. "Come stay with us."

She smiles, her eyes still on the ice, head trembling. Then the smile disappears, and she says quietly, "I don't think Bruce would handle that very well." She turns away. "I better go check on him. Make sure he hasn't passed out in the snow."

Inside, Mom is sitting with her elbows propped on the dining room table, the backs of her hands supporting her chin. She looks her sixty-four years and then some. Why is it in times of distress that a person's age really shows? I gently rub her back.

"It's hard to watch that," she says.

"I know."

"I don't know what to do." She rubs her forehead with the palm of her hand.

"We'll think of something," I say. An empty promise, I know.

Dad's never been one to hold back tears, whether from a movie or a beautiful song or news of a dying child. Tonight is no different. He dabs at his eyes with the handkerchief he keeps in his pocket. I lean over the back of the couch and hug him. "Love you, Dad."

"Love you, too, Mike."

"We'll think of something," I say again. He's worn Old Spice for as long as I can remember, and the familiar smell fills my nostrils as I kiss the top of his head.

"I'll kill the bastard," he says.

"We'll think of something," I whisper.

I decide to check on Kelly. It's been fifteen minutes, and she still hasn't come in. I find her out front, sitting on the bed of her pick-up truck, legs swinging over the edge like a little girl. For a moment, I think she's shivering from the cold, but the thought, the wish, quickly leaves, and I realize it's just the shaking. Bruce lies on his side next to Kelly, a thick green blanket covering him. For just a moment, I wonder if she's killed him, but then I hear a loud, muffled snore.

"Remember that pearl?" Kelly asks without looking up.

The question catches me off guard. "The pearl?"

She watches Bruce, listens to his drunken snoring. "I lied about losing it," she says. "I never dropped it. It never fell down a sewer drain."

It's strange how snow can look like stars drifting down from the heavens, stars you've been told your whole life are massive balls of gas and fire. Then they land on your skin, merely pinpricks of cold.

"But Mom said—"

"I know what she said."

"You came home crying. You were all scraped up."

Her eyes shine. She rubs her hand over Bruce's thigh, an act of affection I can't reconcile. "You remember Carl Johanson?"

At first I don't, but then I do. He used to carry packs of Juicy Fruit on him, and when he'd come over, he'd always toss me a pack. "Sure."

"We were making out in the woods behind Jenson's orchard. You know? But—I didn't—I didn't want him to…"

She stops swinging her legs and becomes still.

"Want him to what?" I ask. Then I get it. "Oh." Then I get it some more. "Oh. Jesus."

She leans forward and puts her face in her hands. Her body heaves with sobs. It still hurts to hear someone cry. I put my arm around her. "I'm so sorry. Kelly. Jesus."

"I swallowed it," she says, her voice cracking.

"Swallowed it?"

"The pearl." She looks up. Her eyes are wet polished agates. "I'd never had something so beautiful, and after he left -- I needed something beautiful inside of me."

The entire sky falls in growing white flakes. It melts as soon as it touches us and turns our hair to cold wet straw.

"It went down easily," she says. "I was down on the ground, you know? Rotten apples all around, and sticks poking my arms and knees. I'd never felt so dirty."

She puts her head on my shoulder. "It went down so easily," she says again. "I wanted it to stay inside of me, so every few days I swallowed it again." She looks down at her husband. "He's never seen it."

Maybe it's the darkness, the cold, the hypnotic swirl of snow. Maybe all we need is some light. Some warmth. "Come inside," I say. "It's too cold out here."

"You go ahead. I won't be long."

The way she says it...

Bruce is dead to the world, his tender white throat bare to the elements. I watch Kelly, look in her eyes. Try to see past them into the workings of her mind.

She chuckles. "I'm too damn tired to take an axe to the son of a bitch," she says.

I lean over and hug her tightly. "Okay," I say.

As I go inside, the snow grows heavy and wet, hesitating toward rain. Dad dozes on the couch with the basketball game droning on. I see a strip of light beneath the bathroom door, and hear the slosh of water; Mom's only vice—her nightly bath.

I don't look forward to the drive home. With this weather and the way the roads are, it will take at least an hour. I consider spending the night, but with Corinne and Amanda sick, I should get home and be there for them in the morning. Pretty lousy of me to have left them. I envision Amanda crawling into bed with Corinne, their feverish bodies dampening the sheets, communicating their misery to each other through fits of coughing. But damn it, it's so rare that I see Kelly anymore.

Of course, I wish Bruce had never laid a hand on Kelly. I wish he'd never insulted her or berated her or ignored all of her birthdays. I wish he'd never met my sister. I wish he'd never been born. But I also wish that Mom and Dad hadn't seen him hit her. I wish they could remain ignorant of Kelly's situation and go to sleep believing their children live happy lives. They shouldn't have to spend their golden years worrying about us. I kiss Dad lightly on the forehead, careful not to wake him, then don my coat and gloves. I decide not to disturb Mom, either. I jot a note saying I'll call them in the morning. Maybe we can figure out what to do then. I head out into the cold, damp night, looking for Kelly to say goodbye.

As I walk out to the driveway, I notice two things simultaneously.

One, Kelly's pick-up truck is gone, and two, there's an envelope tucked beneath one of the windshield wipers of my SUV. When I pull it from beneath the wiper and feel the hard lump between my fingers, my heart lodges in my throat. I take off a glove and pull out a smooth, round bead, something I've held only once before.

The largest Mississippi pearl ever found.

Kelly's pearl.

I see her jagged handwriting on the back of a gas receipt that flutters from the envelope like a dead leaf to the ground. I pick it up.

For you, it says. *I don't need it anymore. Love you, little bro.*

Kelly.

I try to swallow my heart back into place. Tire tracks veer off the driveway and cross the lawn to the back of the house. I don't think to go inside and wake up Mom and Dad. I don't think to call 911. I only think to run.

My leather shoes soak through as they splash through the slush of tire tracks. The snow has turned to rain, and the rain feels like cold bullets on the back of my neck. The tracks continue across the back lawn to the lake.

I hear ice pop and groan. Catch a whiff of exhaust. Two bright red eyes in the distance grow slowly smaller. Tail lights. Their glow briefly illuminates the half-sunk shanty less than a hundred yards out. Even at that distance, the crunch of tires on dirty ice is audible over the crackle of icy rain.

I try to scream Kelly's name, but there's nothing in me, no air. I struggle to fill my lungs, to suck oxygen from the rain-drenched atmosphere. My throat burns.

If the ice can hold a pick-up truck, it can hold me.

I step out onto the ice. Slip and fall. But I find my voice. "Kelly!"

I rise, soaked and freezing, and force myself to run again. "Kelly!"

Brake lights glow fiercely as the truck stops. A figure sits up slowly in the truck bed. In the hellish reflection of red light, I recognize Bruce's sodden shape.

My foot breaks through the ice and the freezing black water feels like sharp fingernails digging into my shin.

I've never felt so desperate, so helpless. This can't be happening. This isn't real, is it? I have to save her.

I pull my leg from the hole and limp forward.

Bruce falls off the pick-up bed and lays immobile, face up on the ice. I see the back of Kelly's head silhouetted against the glow of the dashboard. She sits in the driver's seat completely still. Even her shaking has stopped.

I stumble, slide, lurch and run. The truck is thirty yards away. "Get out," I yell. The pearl is hard and cold against my thigh, pressing through the wet pocket of my jeans.

Kelly's head turns slightly.

"Please," I whimper.

I hear a click. A truck door opening. But it opens only an inch. I hear a loud groan, pitiful, awful, and at first I think it's Bruce regaining consciousness. Kelly must hear it, too, because the truck door clicks again, and I realize Kelly's shut herself back in. The groan grows louder, inhuman, and I stop as I realize it's not coming from Bruce. It's the ice.

With a sharp crack, the walls of the half-sunk shanty split and collapse. Its mass rises, shifts, then disappears from the surface. Kelly's eyes shine briefly in the rearview mirror, two glistening pearls infinitely more perfect and pure than the thing in my pocket. She lifts her hand and waves to me, slowly. Then with a dull splintering noise I'll never forget, a noise I still hear when everything else is silent, the truck jerks forward and down. Bruce rolls in after it and disappears.

I stop running, and when I scream, it doesn't even sound like me. The blood in my veins feels like slivers of hot glass. I'm frozen in place. I have to help her. I can't help her. That's Kelly, that's my sister. Oh God Kelly what did you do, what were you thinking, *why did you drive out onto the ice?*

Swim. Kelly, swim. Get out of the truck and swim.

Maybe she's swimming to the surface. Maybe right now she's swimming to the surface and she's going to get out and she's going to be okay. I can still see the faint glow of tail and brake lights beneath the surface. Maybe she's—

I hear something, like birch-wood popping in a hot fire. I realize it's the ice cracking beneath me. The entire surface swells as if the lake is breathing.

I don't know what to do. What can I do?

Oh God, Kelly.

I find myself slowly backing up.

The taillights fade beneath the heaving ice.

I want to lie down. Curl up in a ball and suck my thumb. I fear my body will never stop trembling. My fingers are raw and stiff. What can I do?

I keep backing up. Why can't I stop? Why can't I force myself forward? Why can't I save my sister? I keep backing up until the ice stops moving, until the black and gray horizon becomes still.

What can I do?

I slide the pearl out from the cold wet folds of my pocket. I kiss it. Hold it up against the hazy glow of an emerging moon. It's almost a perfect match.

The rain stops. What can I do?

Sometimes we all need something pure and perfect within us.

So this is what I do.

I tilt back my head, open my mouth and let the pearl drop.

I try to hold onto the memory of Kelly's rare smile and perfect jewel eyes as it slides easily down my throat.

About the Author

Joel Arnold is the author of several novels. His short stories and articles have appeared in dozens of publications, including **Weird Tales, Chizine, American Road Magazine** and the anthologies **Resort To Murder** and **Shivers VII**. In 2010 he received both a MN Artists Initiative Grant as well as the Speculative Literature Foundation's Gulliver Travel & Research Grant.

Contact him via **email:** joelarnold@mchsi.com

Check out his **blog:** http://authorjoelarnold.blogspot.com

Sign up for Joel's **newsletter:** http://eepurl.com/Gre2f